DJ

OUT FOR BLOOD

B. MILLER

B. MILLER

For permission requests, write to the author, addressed:
"Attention: Permissions Coordinator", at the address below.
Infinity Publications, LLC.
Vanderbilt Media House, LLC.
999 Waterside Drive
Suite 110
Norfolk, VA 23510
(804)286-6567

Infinity Publications

www.vanderbiltmediahouse.net
Library of Congress Control Number: 2022913258
ISBN-13 : 978-1-953096-31-9
First Edition : March 2023
10 9 8 7 6 5 4 3 2 1

This book was printed in the United States

ACKNOWLEDGEMENTS

I would like to first thank God for giving me the strength and mindset to write this book. Next, I want to thank my parents for always having my back through thick and thin. I love you and dedicate this book to both of you. I want to give thanks to my best friend/manager Alvertina Brooks for your support, push, and helping me get my books published. I thank Nicole, Nae, Sea, Kwashawnda, Kimaria, Taejah, Jackie, and Heaven, who are all very special to me. I love each of you.

Shout out to Santana, Joe, Chris, Jay-O, Ray, Jig, My MGB family, Bino, Slim, Bundles, Rodneyke, and everyone who showed me love and support over the years. RIP Tyresha Walker. You will be forever missed but never forgotten. I love you!!!

Chapter 1
DJ

"Jackson! Inmate Jackson! Pack your lil dirty ass up. How are you not gonna be awoken on your release date? You must like it here," Officer Hicks said, standing at DJ's cell door.

"Dirty?" DJ said and scratched his head over his black doo rag.

"I know your lil funky ass ain't calling me dirty?" DJ scratched his nappy beard and rubbed his eyes until they focused. He looked over at the petite woman and smiled. She smiled back, revealing her little gold crown over her deaden gray tooth.

"I knew you liked it here. You ain't trying to go home nigga."

"Naw, I popped a shit load of pills last night because I would not have gotten no sleep if I hadn't popped 'em. 'Ya heard me?"

"You're a damn junkie," she said with DJ firing back.

"Yeah, but you want me. You know you do. I truly apologize for not being able to dig up in that lil ass like these other niggas did."

"Well, you're about to go home. So, what's up?" She asked, twirling her loose hair weave on her fingers.

"Write your number down," DJ replied.

"I already did," she grinned, going into her uniform shirt to pull it out of her bra.

DJ grabbed the card with her phone number and made his way out of the cell. He then proceeded to the pod and dapped up a few people who were out playing poker, including his cellmate.

"Be easy and stay out there mane. This shit here is for the birds.

Remember niggas like me who ain't never going home. Take advantage of this chance my nigga because everybody doesn't get a second chance." His old cellmate said sincerely.

"Fa'sho my nigga. Be easy," DJ said.

"Look, do you wanna leave or not?" Officer Hicks interrupted.

It took about fifteen minutes for DJ to get processed out of prison, but those fifteen minutes seemed like an eternity to him. He was all but overwhelmed with anxiety after eight years of hell. His stomach was full of butterflies, while his armpits and palms were full of sweat. Quickly, he pinched himself to ensure that this wasn't one of his many recurring dreams for the thousandth time.

DJ found his mother and daughter waiting as he walked into the lobby. His heart pounded against his chest as his daughter ran to him. It was by far the best feeling he had ever felt.

"Daddy, Daddy, Daddy!" she hollered out, jumping into his arms.

"Daddy, are you coming home with us? Can we stop at McDonald's on the way home?" she asked, firing off question after question before he could even respond to the first one.

"Hold on, baby, slow down. We can go anywhere you want to go."

"YES!" she exclaimed.

His mother stood there smiling with signs of decades-old stress evident from the new gray hairs peeping through her original black hair color and not to mention the puffy bags below her eyes. The intense love for this tiny woman overwhelmed him as he blamed himself for the immense signs of fatigue and stress he witnessed. He promised himself that instead of being a burden, he'd return the favor by comforting her this time. He hugged her tightly as his daughter grabbed onto both of them. It was at the very moment when he knew it was happening. He was finally free, and his reoccurring nightmares were now over. He placed his arms around them and headed for the exit leaving the pits of hell to start a new life. As soon as he got outside the gate, he removed Officer Hicks's phone number from his shirt pocket. He then balled it up, hurling it on the ground.

"What's that, daddy?" Neek asked.

"Oh, that was nothing, baby. Just some trash in my pocket," DJ replied, eyeing the paper before picking it back up. *Hell, this shit might come in handy later on down the road.*

"Come on y'all. Let's get outta here. I've been here long enough," DJ told his family.

Chapter 2
DANA

"Tracy! Tra-cy!"

"What, Dana!? Can't you see that a bitch trying to sleep? Damn!"

"Get your ass up! I told you to stay over here so we can go to the mall before it gets crowded. Not so your ass can sleep all damn day. So, get up!" Dana yelled, snatching the covers from her best friend.

"You know that DJ got out yesterday, and I wanna go get something sexy to wear to the club for him tonight." Dana fussed.

"Cut it out, Dana. You don't even know if he's gonna be there and you in here trippin'." Tracy replied, still half asleep.

"Girl, you know Trill is going to be there too, just like he is every other weekend, and being that he and DJ are like brothers, DJ's going to be with him. Plus, I saw Trill the other day, and he told me they would be at the Hyper Link tonight."

Dana threw Trill's name in on purpose, knowing that Tracy was head over heels for the nigga even though he hadn't noticed her in like forever. But just like she thought...it was enough to get Tracy out of bed.

"Girl, I ain't even trippin' off of no Trill, with is fine ass," Tracy said.

"Um hmm. Girl, you're sprung off of that nigga, and he only hit it once." Dana shot back. Tracy thought back to the night Trill had given her a blunt to hit after the club, then left like he didn't know her once he finished smoking. Dana had cursed her out for selling herself so short, so she never told Dana that she and Trill had run into each other a few days later and started somewhat talking.

"Dana, you got some nerve to talk. You haven't even seen DJ since you was fifteen years old. He might not even remember your ass." Tracy said, going into the bathroom.

"Oh, he knows who I am! I wrote him a few times and sent him pictures so he wouldn't forget who...I...am."

Dana left out the part of DJ not writing her back, and for the life of her she just couldn't figure out why a man in prison wouldn't write a woman back. At first, she thought he might be gay, but she knew deep in her heart that her boo went too hard for that. She wasn't arrogant, but who wouldn't want a peanut butter complexion, 5'4" tall, true to life, ride or die chick?

She got a nice ass, voluptuous C-cup breasts and could pass for Indian or a Butter Pecan Rican Mami with Dom Perignon taste and class. *Maybe he just hadn't gotten any of my letters. Damn*! She cursed under her breath.

Who am I kidding? Davon Jackson, aka DJ is not even thinking 'bout me.

DJ was 18 years old when he got locked up and not to mention one of the craziest niggas she's ever had known. DJ was in prison on trumped up murder charges, and everyone knew that. The police wanted him off the streets so badly that they planted fake evidence on him. On top of that, he was fine as hell with a capital "F."

They even paid people to testify against him. The prosecutors didn't want to take a chance of him beating the case and offered him an eight-year plea deal for manslaughter, which DJ took once the police had set the trap in motion. Now he's back, and Dana is no longer a little girl. She just hoped he didn't get back with his no-good baby momma.

"Trifling Bitch!" she spat out loud.

"Dana? Dana? Girl, you have lost your damn mind! What the hell are you doing standing in the middle of the hallway, looking at the wall, talking to your damn self?" Tracy asked.

"Whatever bitch! Ain't nobody talking to their damn selves! Anyway, are you ready yet?" Dana asked, changing the subject.

"You're slow as shit damn!" Dana said, playing it off that she was indeed thinking about DJ.

"Damn, Dana! Hold on! The mall is not going anywhere. Can I at least put my shoes on?" Dana looked at Tracy and rolled her eyes.

"Well, lock the door on your way out." Dana fussed, walking out of the apartment to start the car.

Dana was born LaDana Davis and was the child of a small dope pusher father and dope fiend mother. Her parents wanted her to have a better life than they had as she grew up. Her father spoiled her with money he made on the streets, while her mother kept her up on the game regarding the streets' dos and don'ts. Dana's mother kept her head buried deep into her schoolbooks even though she was strung out on drugs.

Her mother wanted to get off drugs badly to ensure that her daughter succeeded in finishing school. But the monkey on her back would prove to be stronger than her and crawled back on her until she surrendered to it and began using drugs again. They did all that they could for their daughter. They loved her the best way they knew and went to their premature deaths, wondering if they had done enough for her.

Dana had taken in everything they had taught her and finished school. She was hoping to start college next fall and take up business management, but the few grand her father left behind weren't going to cover her tuition. So, she worked full-time at a soul food restaurant until something better came along.

Tracy McNair and Dana had become best friends after the death of Dana's parents. Tracy's mother had taken Dana in. They were like night and day, though. Tracy was fast and into the street life, trying to find a baller to cater to her every need, and if a guy gave her the right amount, a quickie was on the menu.

Dana, on the other hand, was only into her books and used the same formula as Tracy, only she applied her hunt consistently to make things happen for herself instead of waiting on some baler to appear. She had never even had a real boyfriend, let alone slept with one. She still hoped that someday DJ would notice her and be her first real everything, then Tracy would stop trying to drag her out to the clubs every weekend and hook her up with some fake baller. Even though, at times, Dana was tempted to go out with one of the ballers but still refused.

DJ...Out for Blood

Chapter 3
DJ

Damn, this nigga was taken all day, DJ thought. Trill had called him over an hour ago, saying that he was on the way over, and now DJ was getting bored waiting for him to show up. DJ's mother and daughter had left early in the morning, leaving him in bed. The whole day he had spent with them the day before had worn him out. Trill had wanted him to come to hang out, but since it was his first day home, he decided to kick back with the family. Now that he had decided to hang, Trill took all day to pick him up.

DJ grew tired of sitting in the house and went to sit on the porch waiting. So much had changed in the neighborhood since he had been gone. People had moved away, some killed and locked up, and the other guys his age were replaced by younger crews or 'sets' as they are now known. Now houses that were brand new when he got locked up are run down.

Outside of that, not much by way of the hustle had changed. He still lived on Richmond City's Northside, right across the street from Providence Park, where everything was still hustle and flow. The park was jumping, which was evident from his front-row seat on the porch. Drug deals were going down while guys played basketball on the two full courts, females stood around trying to look cute, and dope feigns ran back and forth to cars that pulled up alongside the park to buy drugs. Yep, he was definitely back home! Just as he was about to go back inside to give Trill another call, he heard his name being called and turned around just in time to see Trill's slim linky ass bending the corner.

"Damn nigga, where the love at? I haven't seen you in six years," Trill said, giving DJ some dap and hug.

"Nigga, what the hell took you so long?" DJ asked.

"Look at you, fussing already," Trill replied, laughing. DJ took a step back to have a better look at this little nigga while fussing.

"Man, I've been waiting here for over an hour, and you're just getting here!" Trill looked at DJ smiling with a mouth full of gold teeth before he answered.

"Dawg, I've been here the whole time. That's my car right there." Trill pointed at a brand new all-black Lexus GS 300 with limo-tinted windows sitting on twenty-inch rims.

"I just had to run to the park to make a few more dollars so we can do it up tonight, but I'm ready now, so let's roll."

DJ wanted to put his foot up Trill's ass for making him wait, but instead, he asked, "What's up for tonight?"

"We're going to Hyper Link," Trill responded after pressing the unlock alarm of his car. "Your boys are doing a show tonight."

"My boys? Who the hell are you talking about?" DJ asked, getting into the car, but Trill pulled off before responding.

"O.C.U nigg! Dream, Slim, and Swift. Slim made sure you got V.I.P, so you don't have to pay for shit. This is your night nigga! Oh yeah, your girl going too. She stays asking about your ass."

DJ gave Trill a sharp stare knowing he couldn't have heard him right even though he knew he did.

"Yo Trill, stop playin' with me. You know I don't deal with Shay! I can't stand that BITCH!"

"Aww damn, Trill, I know you didn't tell her I was home." Trill burst into laughter while noticing there wasn't anything funny on DJ's face.

"Ain't nobody talking about your damn baby momma nigga. I'm talking about Dana."

Hearing Trill speak Dana's name sent DJ into a quick daze as they pulled up in front of D.T.L.R shoe store.

"Come on, dawg. Get whatever you want," Trill said, snapping DJ out of his daze.

DJ couldn't help but think about her. She had written him a few times and sent him pictures while he was in prison. But he never wrote back. He couldn't front she was beautiful, but she was a little girl when he left. Only fifteen years old and like a little sister to him. He knew she always had a crush on him before he got locked up, but he thought it would pass with time.

Two years into his bid, she started writing, talking about waiting for him to come home. He didn't know what to say, so he never wrote back.

DJ followed Trill into the store and grabbed a pair of Air Force One's with a Coogie outfit, throwing them onto the counter along with Trill's new gear. After Trill paid for the clothes. Together they walked out of the store to prepare for the night to fall in the city.

Chapter 4
DJ

DJ and Trill arrived downtown on Franklin Street around ten o'clock at night, and things were in full stride. Traffic was backed up for blocks on the one-way street. There were groups of people on both sides of the street who were trying to be seen. Herds of people were sitting in cars and some on top of them.

"Damn, Trill. Since when does Franklin Street jump like this?" DJ asked, sitting on the passenger side, looking fresh too death in the Lexus GS 300. He saw the sign to the club up ahead and wanted everybody to know he was home.

"Yo, stop the car. I wanna walk the rest of the way. I'll meet you out front." DJ jumped out of the car and started walking before it completely stopped.

"Fo'sho my nig. Let 'em know you're back. I'll be at the door waiting for you." Trill yelled out of the window. DJ was seeing people he hadn't seen in years. While taking the short walk down the strip, it was as if he'd never left. Everywhere he turned, niggas gave him dap with money folded in their hands, talking about how they had missed him. *YEAH RIGHT!* They would have gotten at him when he was still in the can if it were really like that, but it was all good. He knew how the game went. All he wanted right now was to pick up one of the women on his jack to take to a hotel after the club. Up the street, he could see Trill headed towards him as he took his time absorbing everything and everybody around him.

DJ...Out for Blood

"Nigga, where you going?" Trill asked as they met up, giving DJ a dumb look. "Damn, you've been gone too long. We don't do the standing in lines shit!"

Trill pushed through the crowd, walking into the club as if he owned it with DJ behind him. To DJ's surprise, the bouncers let them pass, welcoming him home. DJ stopped to take in all the sights as he walked into the club. To his right sat a small lounge area with three couches and six tables. The bar sat on his left where he headed, and the dance floor was straight ahead on the club's lower level. Since he didn't dance, he chose to hang out at the bar for a while. Most likely, the dance floor was where he'd be able to find Trill, who had left him standing by it.

DANA

Dana had just walked through a side door behind the bar from the dancing floor when she noticed DJ standing by the front door looking lost. DJ had a yellow and white fitted hat turned backward on his head with braids hanging out of the sides, which was done up fresh and crisp matching his yellow Coogie shirt. *Damn, that nigga is sexy!* She thought.

She watched DJ take a final look around before walking his six-foot frame to the bar, still not noticing her, and ordering himself a drink. She looked down at his shoes to see what kind he had on, and like she thought she'd find a fresh pair of all-white Air Force ones to compliment his blue and yellow Coogie jeans.

She damn near ran off the dance floor to talk to DJ, but now that she was so close to him, she was nervous. Trill had told her that he was up here, and up to this point, she couldn't wait to holla at him after so long, now she didn't know what to say. "Fuck it!" she thought. She called his name as she reached out to touch his shoulder.

"DJ?"

DJ...Out for Blood

DJ

DJ felt someone tap on his shoulder as he turned around and stood eye to eye with Dana. 'Damn, she's so beautiful.' DJ was lost for words at first.

"What's good, shawdy?' he finally asked.

"You're what's good." She responded, looking up into his brown eyes before taking a seat at the bar. She wanted to run her fingers across his smooth brown skin and press her full lips against his.

"Oh yeah, so what are you drinking?" DJ asked, pulling out the small knot of money he had accumulated since touching down. "Better yet, get us a table so we can talk."

Dana walked off and stopped a few feet away to see if DJ was watching her. He had to laugh. He was cold busted, but who wouldn't be watching an ass like that crammed into a one-piece body suit. Not to mention the additional switch the heels gave her.

Another tap on his shoulder brought him out of his thoughts of Dana and put him back on point. His whole night was going to turn upside down when he turned around and noticed his daughter's mother, Shay.

"What the fuck do you want?" He growled out of his clenched teeth.

"Hey baby, when did you get out?" She asked, trying to kiss him on the lips. DJ mushed her face so hard that she almost fell backward and would have if it wasn't for the guy next to her catching her just in time.

"Nigga! What the hell is wrong with you?" Shay yelled, looking like she wanted to charge at him with nails flying, but decided against it and walked off, muttering threats.

Trill came through the crowd with a bottle of Moët, laughing. DJ watched her walk off, then looked to see if Dana had seen the altercation. She nodded at him and smiled to let him know she had seen everything.

"I see you found your future wife," Trill teased as DJ ordered his drink and left him standing at the bar without responding.

DJ...Out for Blood

DANA

Dana watched as DJ walked toward her and couldn't help but blush. He was so fine that just his smile alone did something to her. The way she watched him handle his daughter's mother told her the relationship was over between them, which she was glad of because she couldn't stand Shay.

Soon as DJ reached the table where Dana was waiting, the club put the spotlights on him. She looked up and saw O.C.U on stage, ready to perform.

"This song is for you, nigga!" Dream yelled into the mic pointing over to DJ.

Put tha gun to ya/

Put tha, Put tha gun to ya/

let it sing you a song.

The crowd went wild as the group spit the lyrics to the hook. Dana looked over to DJ, watching him enjoying the music. One minute everything was good, then the next minute, DJ went diving over the table, landing on top of her as gunshots rang out. No sooner than they hit the floor, Dana felt all her wind escape, knocking her unconscious and surrendering her unconscious.

DJ

"Trill! Trill!" DJ called out, doing his best to peel around the table as bullets whizzed past, trying not to catch a stray one. He raised off Dana a little to make sure she was alright when he noticed a small pool of blood forming around her. One second, he had been standing in the spotlight, feeling the moment of being a free man. The next second, DJ was ducking bullets.

"Nigga she's dead! Let's go!" Trill yelled, grabbing DJ's arm to pull him out of harm's way.

"Snap out of it, dawg! You're fresh out. We need to bounce before Five-O gets here!" DJ snapped back to reality, jumped up, and followed Trill out of the club when he heard Trill mention the cops. Trill jumped into the Lexus and threw the passenger's side door open.

"Get in. Let's go!" Trill roared.

"Damn, I can't believe Dana got hit, man Fuck!" DJ shouted, getting into the car.

"Better her than you. Fuck that bitch!"
Trill said while speeding through traffic. He pulled over a few blocks away.

"Give me your shit," he told DJ.

DJ never noticed the blood splatter on his shirt until he took it off to give to Trill, who then threw the shirt into a dumpster in the back of some apartments. DJ rode in silence for the rest of the ride, unsure how he was supposed to feel. He had never told Trill that he had started developing feelings for Dana through her letters. Trill was his lil homie from the back in the day before he got locked up and was the only one who kept in touch with him and ensured his family was okay. He had told Trill how Dana felt about him, but he kept quiet about how he really felt about her.

"You a'ight dawg?" Trill asked, pulling up in front of his crib.

"Yeah, I'm good. I'll holla at you Monday once I get back from visiting my P.O. I'mma chill with my family tomorrow, but you can come through if you get the time." With that said, DJ got out of the car and closed the door, still thinking about Dana.

Chapter 5
DJ

DJ got up at eight o'clock Monday morning, still tired from spending the day before with his mother and daughter. His whole day had been going well until Trill stopped by and told him that the bullets hitting Dana was meant for him, so his entire mood changed.

"It was a botched hit. What saved you was the fact that Dana had taken the hit on you. Right now, she's in a coma but still alive," Trill expressed.

DJ called a cab to take him to see his parole officer. As he rode in the backseat, he decided after his meeting that he would walk the five blocks to M.C.V. Hospital to see Dana afterward.

As he walked inside the court building, DJ could tell it wasn't a regular court building. Everything about it screamed F.E.D.'s. He couldn't explain it, but it seemed as if the cool air was more relaxed than in the regular court buildings, including the guards' clothes.

Five officers sat behind a metal detector with grey slacks, red ties, white shirts, and blue blazers that didn't do much to conceal the guns on their hips. A Morgan Freeman look-alike walked up and requested identification.

"ID, please? Take everything out of your pockets, place them into the tray and walk through the metal detector, please," he asked DJ, then handing him back his prison I.D. although he was being polite, all of his comrades kept their hands on their guns until DJ complied.

"Where are you going, sir?" Morgan Freeman's twin asked.

"The Probation Office," DJ replied.

"Second floor," he said before returning to the desk, reclaiming his seat. DJ made it to the probation office without complications. He followed the instructions from the receptionist stating where he was to sign in and took a seat. Soon as he sat down, a U.S. Marshal walked into the room, looking at DJ and asking for a Terrell Fields. DJ was nervous as hell as the thoughts of returning to prison flooded his mind.

"Naw, I'm D. Jackson," DJ answered.

"Well, then, you must be Fields?" The other guy, the U.S. Marshal was referring to, jumped up and made a quick dash for the door, only to be tripped up and slammed to the floor. DJ couldn't blame him for trying to run even though he had no place to go. The building was locked up tighter than Fort Knox. DJ sat there wondering if they were coming back for him. Before the U.S. Marshal called him, he breathed a sigh of relief, knowing that his visit was only for a urine test.

DJ didn't want to cause any trouble but couldn't help but wonder if the guy giving the urine test was gay because the whole time he was trying to piss, the guy had his eyes locked in on his penis. DJ decided to keep quiet to avoid going back to prison for something stupid.

It took DJ almost ten minutes to walk from the courthouse to the hospital. Five minutes to fill out the forms and another three to find Dana's room, where he sat watching her sleep peacefully. Even in a coma, she's beautiful, he thought to himself.

"I'm so glad somebody has finally come to see her." DJ turned around to find the nurse standing behind him. DJ was lost in his thoughts, so he didn't hear the nurse walk into the room. "What do you mean somebody *finally* came to her?" DJ knew what she meant. He just wanted to hear her say that Dana's no good ass friends hadn't stopped by to see her.

"May I need to ask who you are before I go into any details?"

"I'm her fiancé," DJ said without thinking.

"Oh, ok," she said, smiling.

"Well, she has been here for two days already, and nobody has come to check on her. We only knew who she was because she had her ID in her pocket. The police went to the address on her ID, but nobody was home."

That made DJ think, *why hadn't any of Dana's friends visited her, especially Tracy?*

"Here, take my number," DJ voiced, searching for something to write with. Then he remembered the pen he had stolen from the Probation office.

"Do you mind giving me a lil time alone with her?" DJ asked, handing her his phone number.

"Sure, but not too long, hospital policy."

"If you need anything, just hit the button on the side of the bed. It comes directly to this pager," the nurse said, pointing to the side of her hip where it was attached. She then smiled at DJ as she walked out the door.

DJ scooted the chair closer to the bed and grabbed Dana's hand. He didn't know if it was true, but people said a person could hear people talking to them when in a coma.

"Dana, I'm sorry about what happened, but I promise you, I will get revenge in your honor. Death to all those who has hurt you!
I just have to find out who they are first," he whispered.

Once he finished talking to Dana, he made two calls. One was to Trill to scoop him up, and the other was to an old head with whom he had left a few things to hold before he went to prison. While he sat and waited on Trill, he finished watching Dana sleep. Once again, trying to figure out why nobody had come by to be with Dana but him. He knew why her parents hadn't because they were both dead. Her pops had been killed in a shoot-out with the FEDS when they raided his dope house, then two months later, her mother overdosed.

Dana's best friend Tracy's mother had taken her in and raised her as her own so she wouldn't have to go into the foster care system. From what he had heard, Tracy's mother had died of cancer about a month ago, and he couldn't help but wonder where Tracy was.

Chapter 6
Trill

"DJ!" You're trippin' dawg!" Trill exclaimed. He couldn't believe that DJ had them lying up under a filthy ass porch in Church Hill on the city's East End, waiting for the owner to come home, which they had been there for a while. The house belonged to a guy named Travon, better known as Tee, who was the brother of the guy DJ was accused of killing and the owner of the botched hit that had almost killed Dana. What Tee didn't know was that DJ wasn't the person who had killed his brother. He was just the fall guy. But now, DJ had every intention of paying Tee back for the surprise hit. Trill had given DJ the information he learned about the hit and Tee's location on the ride home from the hospital. After hearing that and then stopping at old head Jessie's house, they formulated a strategic plan.

Now here they were, just lying under Tee's front porch, waiting to catch him off guard by surprise or to kidnap his son and girlfriend just in case Tee came home with a few of his boys and couldn't get to him right then. It didn't matter which one, long as one of them happened before the night was over. Trill was strapped with an SKS assault rifle with a 75-round banana clip, while DJ held on to two .357 magnum revolvers.

"Nigga, just chill and be patient," DJ mumbled back. No sooner than those words left his mouth, a red Lexus LS 400 pulled up. They could see two heads in the car's front seat but couldn't tell if someone was in the back because of the dark tint. Two men exited the vehicle a moment later and walked towards the house, laughing and talking loudly. When they reached the first five steps to the house, DJ's heart started racing, thumping hard against his chest. He wasn't scared, not even a little. He was excited to get in his first kill within six years. Once Tee reached the third step, DJ quietly climbed from beneath the porch, cocking back both hammers simultaneously.

"Don't move! Don't even think about it!" DJ said in a low, serious tone. Trill climbed out from the other side of the porch, now coming around with the SKS pointed at their backs. DJ slowly walked towards Tee and his boy while they mean mugged him, smacking them one at a time with the barrel of his gun, knocking them both unconscious.

"Shit!" DJ cursed as one of the guns went off in the process.

"Check them niggas for guns," DJ told Trill as he walked to the front door. Tee's girl opened the door, trying to be nosey, thinking it was Tee and his boys acting a fool. But when she saw DJ instead, she tried to slam the door back closed quickly, but he blocked it, snatching her out of the house. DJ smacked her with such force across the face that she staggered a little before dropping to her knees while remaining conscious.

"Damn!" DJ thought, "she's tougher than both of them niggas."

"They clean," Trill said after duct taping Tee and his boy.

"A'ight, throw me the tape," DJ said, grabbing the girl by her weave.

"Please let me go! Please!" she started to beg.

"Bitch, shut the fuck up before I smoke your lil ass! If you wanna live, I advise you to do what I say and keep quiet."

Before she even got a chance to respond, DJ smacked her with the bottom of his gun, rendering her unconscious this time, with two of her front teeth now missing.

As Trill dragged Tee and his boy into the house, DJ started duct taping Tee's girl's hands and feet before picking her up and throwing her into the front door. Trill proceeded to check the house, ensuring nobody else was there, before going into the kitchen to get a pot of ice cold water.

"Ain't this some shit! These niggas are two ballers and don't even have a dining room set," he said, chuckling to himself before leaving the room.

The living room had an all-white couch, a big TV, and nothing else. It was the type of house a baller would have in case the FEDs came calling. Trill came back into the room holding the hand of a lil boy about nine or ten years old. The boy looked so much like Tee that he had to be his son.

"Tell me where the money is, and I might kill you quick. Hold out, and I'mma make you watch me cut your girl to pieces, then your son, and then your boy over there before circling back to you. It won't be pretty either, believe that." DJ said, stooping down in between Tee and his boy.

"Aye yo, playboy? Playboy?" DJ uttered in between smacks to the face of Tee's homeboy, trying to wake him up. Tee's son watched in horror with watery eyes as Trill sat his father up against the sofa and ripped the tape from his mouth. The water hadn't worked on him as it had on everyone else.

"Your time is ticking, dawg, so what's it gonna be? Trill asked, chuckling again. Tee looked as if he were trying to see through the mask of his attackers.

"What's good dawg? What do you want? I don't have no money!" Tee said.

"For starters, I want you to understand that you, I gotta have, but it's up to you how wifey and the seed turn out," DJ replied. "I gotta have you!"

"Why you gotta have me? I haven't done shit to you. I don't even know you dawg," Tee wailed.

DJ could see the shock on his face at the realization that, for him, it was over. DJ stood up and started pacing back and forth around the living room before responding.

"Why do *I* have to have you?

"This stupid ass nigga wanna know why do I have to have *him?* Trill, let's show him why I must have him!" DJ laughed as he pulled off his mask to reveal himself. Tee's eyes got as big as golf balls when he saw that it was DJ behind the mask.

"D... D... DJ, man, it's not even like that," Tee stuttered.

"You killed my brother. What did you expect me to do?" he asked.

"Okay, now which one is it because now I'm confused. It's not like that, or I killed your brother, so it is like that? As a matter of fact, forget the explanation because it doesn't matter. I can't leave you alive. It just boils down to if you go solo or with the company in your presence. It's your choice. Now, where's the money?"

"Tee? Tee? Baby, what's going on? " His girl asked after listening to DJ talk.

"Bitch, if you're not tryna die, I suggest you shut the fuck up and play the background," DJ yelled, tired of playing games with Tee.

"Come on, DJ man. Let my family go. They don't have shit to do with this," Tee begged. "Truth is, it ain't no stash..." Before he could finish his sentence, DJ pulled back the hammer on his gun and pointed it at the head of Tee's son. Mona quickly yelled out.

"It's in the back of my son's closet! Please don't hurt him!" She hollered out, trying to keep from crying.

"Mona, what the fuck you tell him for?" Tee yelled.
In his mind, he felt that as long as he had the money, DJ wouldn't kill him, not knowing that the money was just an extra bonus. His life was what DJ came after.

"Thanks Mona!" DJ said sarcastically to her. '"Trill, go get that! Oh yeah!"

BLAH!

DJ squeezed the trigger, splattering lil Tee's brains all over his living room wall. Trill was caught off guard and jumped at the sound of hearing the gun going off, while Mona began throwing up and crying hysterically.

Tee was in shocked as he stared in disbelief, telling himself that DJ did not just shoot his son.

DJ...Out for Blood

"Nooo! What da fuck! What da fuck, man! I thought you said you were gonna let my family go!" Tee screamed out, trying to regain his composure.

DJ smiled wickedly at the smoking gun before he answered.

"I was, but then I thought about how mine is in a coma laid up in the hospital because of you. Then to make matters worse, you lied about the stash."

"Nigga, that shit is not the same, and you know it! You just killed my son! My son!" Tee finally decided to let his anger show. He couldn't hold it in no more.

"That was my son! Not some funky ass bitch I was fucking? On top of that, your people ain't dead! She's in da fucking hospital still alive!" Tee yelled, squirming around on the floor, trying to break free of the duct tape on his feet and around his wrists, bounding him together. He was trying to get to his now deceased son.

"It doesn't matter if she's still alive. The point is she could be dead and being that I'm the only family she has makes me responsible for her, nigga!"

"Yo, DJ! It's four trash bags full of money and dope back here!" Trill yelled, excited about what he found.

"Two of them are filled with cash. The other two bags are full of work in them." Trill continued as he started dragging all four bags down the hallway.

"A'ight, that's what's up! Take them to the car and bring me that can of gas in the trunk," DJ replied while sticking a fresh piece of tape over Tee's mouth to shut him up.

Once Trill left, DJ went into the bathroom to get a bottle of alcohol, not expecting to find a razor, but there they were. A six packet of Gillette razors sitting right next to the alcohol.

"Homeboy, look what I got for you?" DJ conveyed to Tee as he returned to the living room, sitting the alcohol in front of him.

"Now, this is where the fun starts!" DJ said with a mischievous grin as he pulled Tee's pants down as far as they would go. He grabbed Tee's shriveled penis through the slit in his boxer shorts and put two quick slashes across it before pouring alcohol over it.

Tee tried to scream, but the tape that covered his mouth wouldn't allow it. It sounded more like the billowing of a black smith's airbag than a real scream with snot rushing from his nose and his eyes bulging from the pain. Tee squealed and squirmed around on the floor, trying his best to escape from DJ while Mona watched in horror.

"Now you wanna cry, huh bitch?" DJ spat out at a helpless Tee.

"You should've thought of the consequences before you came fucking 'wit a nigga like me. What? You don't got nothing to say now, huh?" DJ smacked him with the pistol again.

"Yo, DJ!" Trill called to him as he returned to the house with the gas can.

"A'ight, cool. Leave it right there. I'll be out in second." DJ grabbed the gas can and started splashing gas all over the house.

"You wanna know something funny, Tee? I didn't kill your faggot ass brother! All of this shit could have been avoided if your dumb ass had just listened and believe me when I tell you...again!" DJ slapped Tee's boy once again, trying to wake him up.

"Welp, I guess your boy is just gonna wake up dead," DJ said, laughing at himself.

"Oh well, I guess this is one ride he's not trying to take with you, at least not woke anyway." That said, DJ lit the entire matchbook and tossed it over his shoulder on his way out the door.

"I'll see yall niggas in hell!" DJ declared, laughing. No sooner than he jumped into the front seat of the car; the house exploded into flames.

Chapter 7
DJ

A week had passed since the murder of Tee, his homeboy, Mona, and his son. DJ had watched the news daily to confirm the police had no leads. If a person wanted to know something and knew what to look for, then all they had to do was look at the news because they told it all.

After switching cars that night, they returned to DJ's house to split everything down the middle. The first two bags contained six and a half keys of powder coke and twenty-five thousand dollars in one-dollar bills. The other two held just a little over a hundred grand a piece.

Trill left after getting his cut, leaving DJ thinking about moving his mother and daughter the first chance he gets. He had bought the house they currently live in a year before he got knocked off, but now it was time to move them to safer grounds while he was out doing his thing. DJ was deep into his thoughts at the hospital when he felt his hand being squeezed, snapping him back to reality and causing him to jump a little. It wasn't until he looked down that he remembered he had been holding someone's hand.

DJ...Out for Blood

DANA

Dana awoke and looked into the face beside her bed, but she couldn't quite make out the features through her blurred vision. Dana's head was in pain from dehydration. Not to mention her body was stiff and sore. A few minutes passed by before she realized it was DJ causing her to smile.

Quietly, she watched as DJ sat deep in thought, obviously somewhere else, and began to wonder what he was thinking. Just the warmth of him holding her hand and being there gave her comfort and security. Dana used the little strength that she had left and offered his hand a slight squeeze until he came out of his thoughts turning towards her.

She noticed the worried look in his eyes when he turned towards her, but even with the stressful regard he gave her, he still managed to look sexy as hell, and when he finally returned the smile, she thought she'd have an orgasm right there on the spot. She turned away from DJ and looked around the room. Then it all came rushing back that she was in the hospital, but why? She wondered.

DJ

DJ couldn't help but smile when he looked down and saw Dana awoke. She is so beautiful, even under these circumstances, he thought. All his plans of what he would say once she came through went flying out the window, leaving him speechless.

"What happened, DJ?" she asked in a groggy voice.

"Hold on, baby, take it easy. Don't talk. I'mma call the nurse for you." DJ pushed the button beside the bed like the nurse had instructed him to if needed.

"Oh my!" The nurse said when she entered the room. She was surprised to see Dana awake. She paged the doctor and put DJ out once he arrived so they could run some tests on Dana.

DJ walked down to the cafeteria to get a bite to eat while he cleared his mind about things he needed to do. He was sure it was time to stop playing games and make Dana his wifey. DJ always knew that it was going to happen. After almost losing her, he didn't want to take any more chances. He had just wanted to be straight in every sense of the word.

He had two bricks of powder cocaine and just under one hundred twenty grand. Even after finding a nice little place in the county for his mom and daughter, he'd still have enough left to buy a small house somewhere for him and Dana. Then there was the matter of the other four licks he had lined up. The last one hadn't been in the plan, but since Tee had put himself on the menu. There was no need to leave anything valuable behind since he wouldn't need it anymore.

DJ thought about going back upstairs to Dana's room but changed his mind. It was time to get his plans rolling in order, so he'd have to check back with her tomorrow, he thought as he left the hospital. It was already close to seven o'clock in the evening, but by the time he reached home, then back to the South Side, it would be dark, just the way he wanted it.

Chapter 8
DJ

DJ wandered around in the shadows, walking from block to block before finding what he was looking for. He made it home at a quarter to eight, talked to his mother for about ten minutes, threw on his black one-piece jumpsuit, grabbed his pistol grip pump shotgun and a .357 for backup, and was back out the door. DJ had the pump tucked neatly in an open slit sewed into the jumpsuit, giving him easy access to and concealment. He pulled the pump out, taking a few more steps forward before stooping down beside the cars and crawling until he reached a black Delta '88.

Quietly, he patiently waited, watching a guy standing beside the car talk on his cellphone, so deep into his conversation that he didn't even notice DJ as he crept closer. As soon as he turned around to put the key in the door, DJ stood up and cocked the gun, pointing it at him at the same time.

"Don't even think about running, or Im'ma lay your ass right here, so hang up the phone," DJ stated in a low but stern voice while walking around the car. The guy nervously scrambled to press the 'end' button on the cellphone, dropping it to the ground. Then as if on cue, he threw his hands up in the air.

"What can I do for you?" he asked, hoping he didn't get shot.

"First, put your hands down, then put the key in the car door and back the fuck up!"

"Just go ahead and take the car, plus there's $50 in my wallet," the guy offered, doing everything DJ said so he wouldn't get shot. All he could think was... *'That's a big fuckin' gun*!

"Throw the money on the ground," DJ ordered.

"Now lay face down on the ground!"

Soon as the guy bent down to lay on the ground, DJ kicked him in the chin, causing him to grab his mouth with one hand as blood spilled into it and sticking the other one out to signal for DJ to hold on while he begged him not to hit him again. DJ silenced the guy's pleas by smacking him across the head with the pump, knocking him out cold. He took the car keys from out of the door, dragged the guy to the trunk, opened it, and slammed him inside it. DJ bound his feet and hands with the duct tape he'd been wearing on his wrist as a bracelet. He then picked up the 50-dollar bill along with the guy's phone before jumping into the car and pulling off.

As DJ drove to the South Side, he thought about Trill. He had wanted to bring Trill with him for backup, but he quickly thought against it. DJ didn't need Trill knowing his every move. However, if Trill was to go on every lick with him, he would be able to count the money and wouldn't need a connect. It wasn't that he didn't trust Trill because he did. Trill was considered his lil brother.

DJ stayed focused as he took his time driving, using every signal so he wouldn't get pulled over. It was his first time behind the wheel of a car in six years, but just like riding a bike, you'll never forget how. The real problem was that he had somebody in the trunk. A white somebody, which made it even worse than it already was. Hey! What could he say?

He needed a car and didn't know how to pop one up, so he quickly carjacked one. In DJ's mind, the guy is just part of his plan, ultimately becoming a casualty of war in the streets because he was going to die. DJ's number one rule was to rock alone and never leave any witnesses under no circumstances, which he broke when he took Trill along on his last 'adventure,' which is what he refers as his 'robber and murder sprees.' Which was also why he was going to take Trill on his next adventure. If Trill ever got caught by the police, DJ knew he wouldn't be able to snitch on him without first telling on himself. He felt Trill would never snitch on him in his heart, but it was better to be safe than sorry. DJ knew that when niggas start facing heavy time, their lips get loose and start singing in acapella.

When DJ finally made it to Timber Creek apartments without any difficulties, he drove to the back of them and parked by the woods. It was pitch black back there, with none of the apartment buildings facing that street, so he didn't have to worry about being noticed by anyone looking out of a window.

DJ cut the engine off after hitting the automatic trunk opener button inside of the glove compartment. Before exiting the car, he scanned his surroundings to ensure nobody was in the area. Slowly, DJ raised the trunk to ensure the guy didn't somehow get loose from the duct tape. He watched the guy as he lay still unconscious.

SMACK! SMACK!

Without any notice, DJ hit the guy two times across the head.

"That's just in case you thought about waking up," DJ mumbled to the unconscious guy before closing the trunk and walking off. He didn't want the guy to wake up, and somebody just so happened to be walking by while he was moving around in the trunk.

DJ started making his way towards the apartment building he was looking for, staying close to the woods so nobody would see him. All he had to do was make it to the back of the last apartment building, jump up on top of the downstairs apartment's railing and pull himself up to the second floor. It should have been as easy as one, two, or three, but as always, nothing goes as planned. DJ needed that railing to get to the second-floor apartment but cuddled up against the railing were a man and woman. As he got closer to the edge of the apartment building, he could hear people talking in a mellow tone. He crept into the woods and then rounded the corner, finding a tree to peep from behind.

"Casualties of war," DJ mumbled to himself. "Yeah, that's what they're about to be. It's nothing personal to y'all. You gonna just have to understand that y'all was in the wrong place at the wrong time," DJ said as if the couple could actually hear him.

DANA

Dana had laid in the hospital bed, confused, thinking about everything the doctor had just told her. After the doctor had completed tests on her to ensure she was breathing alright and there was no internal bleeding, he informed her that she had been shot twice in the chest and she was lucky to be alive because one of the bullets hit her right under the heart.

"You gave your fiancé quite a scare! I can tell he's a good man, far as I can tell. He stuck by your side the entire time you were in a coma. To be truthful, I think that he's the only one who's been here to see you. Every time I stopped by, he'd be sitting in that chair right there talking to you," the doctor said, pointing at the chair beside the bed.

"Well, I guess I'll let you get your rest, and don't worry. You're excellent. If you need anything, just hit the nurse's call button on the side of your bed.

Dana chuckled as she thought about the doctor calling DJ '*a good man.' If only he really knew DJ, I bet he wouldn't say that shit then*, Dana mumbled, talking to herself. *And little does he know me and DJ are NOT engaged, but it is a good thought*," Dana said, still speaking to herself while smiling at the idea of being engaged to DJ.

"*I wonder what would even make him think that. You know what? I'm not gonna entertain that thought because DJ and I will never be engaged, so I might as well get it out of my mind even if it does sound good.*"

"*Damn, I'm losing my mind sitting here talking to myself. If Tracy's*

42

ass was here, I wouldn't have to be in here talking to my damn self, and why the hell isn't Tracy here anyway?" Dana wondered. *"And where in the hell is DJ? Why hasn't he come back?"* Dana yelled inside her mind.

Dana's mind was running a hundred miles per hour. That last thing that she remembered was being at the club, ready to have drinks with DJ. She didn't know what to think.

"Damn! Damn! Think! What happened next?" she asked herself, talking in the third person. "Think Dana! Think! Ok, let's see. I remember DJ walking over to our table with our drinks after almost knocking his baby momma's head off. O.C.U. had started performing *Put The Gun To Ya*. Tracy pointed at us when Tee pulled out his gun and started shooting at us.

"Oh shit!" Dana's heart started racing as she remembered more and more of what had happened.

"Oh my GOD! I can't believe Tee shot me, and Tracy was with him. I wondered if DJ was here to kill me. He might think that I tried to set him up. Naw! Hell naw! DJ know I wouldn't set him up. He has to know. Shit!"

"This is DJ I'm talking about. He has known me almost my whole life. He knows that I love him and will never cross him, plus I'm the one who almost got killed. Then again, he's also a well-known killer who didn't take kindly to people who crossed him, and if he even thinks a person tried to cross him, he'd dead 'em, but as I said at first, I'm the one who took a bullet not him."

"DJ, my love. You have to believe me," Dana said as if he could hear her. On the one hand, she knew that DJ would kill her, but on the other hand, she felt that he would believe her.

"I just have to talk to DJ, but first, I need to talk to Tracy and hear her story." Dana reached over to grab the phone off the nightstand beside the bed, but two plain-clothes detectives walked into the room before she could dial Tracy's phone number. They both wore black slacks with neatly pressed white shirts. The only difference between the two white detectives were their neckties.

"Ms. Davis?" The detective with the black tie asked.

"Yeah, that's me," Dana answered in irritation as she looked up at him.

"Do you know who shot you or who would want you dead?" he asked as he walked over to her bedside.

"No and no," Dana replied with an attitude, not wanting to be interrogated by no "pigs," as she called them.

"Look, Ms. Davis," the other detective with the red tie with white polka dots on it spoke up.

"I guess this is where y'all supposed to play the good cop, bad cop role, huh?" Dana smirked, cutting him off.

"We can't help you if you don't talk to us," Polka Dot said, finishing his sentence.

"I guess his lil pause was supposed to have scared me," Dana thought as she rolled her eyes at the detectives.

"Look, I didn't ask for y'all's help. I don't need nor want it!" She pressed the nurse button on the side of the bed.

DJ...Out for Blood

"Is everything alright, Ms. Davis?" The nurse asked as she entered the room.

"No, it ain't! These pigs are bothering me. Can you please make them leave?"

"Alright, you two heard her. Ms. Davis needs her rest, so you need to leave." She pointed to the door with urgency. The detectives tried to protest by telling the nurse she was interfering in an ongoing investigation; however, the nurse didn't back down. She fired right back, telling them the hospital could sue them for disturbing a patient under the doctor's care and against the doctor's orders.

"This ain't over Mizz...Davis!" Polka Dot said condescendingly to Dana, reluctantly leaving, giving her the evil eye on his way out. Dana just grinned back at them, nodding her head up and down.

"Are you alright?" the nurse asked.

"The police are just so rude and don't know how to let people get their rest before they start harassing folks."

"Well, if you need me, just push the nurse button again." The nurse left, never giving Dana a chance to answer her question.
Dana tried calling Tracy only to reach her answering machine, so she left her a message to give her a call at the hospital.

Dana put the phone back on the stand, closed her eyes, and started saying a silent prayer for Tracy, scared that she was already dead but hoping she wasn't.

"Dear GOD," Dana began. "Please let my best friend Tracy be alright. She is all I have left in this world, so please protect her. Amen."

Dana felt like being that Tracy wasn't there by her side; she must have already been dead because she knew Tracy would never leave her in the hospital alone.

"Yeah, that must be it. Tracy should know that I know she will never intentionally hurt me or DJ for that matter…at least I hope not."

DJ...Out for Blood

DJ

DJ watched the couple as they kissed and explored each other's bodies for almost ten minutes before they went inside the apartment. They were lucky they had gone inside when they did because while DJ sat back in the woods watching them, he was trying to figure out a way to dead them without using his gun. DJ knew if he had used the gun, he would have alerted unnecessary attention that he didn't want or need. He already had a white man tied up, knocked out cold in the trunk of a car, who might wake up at any time. He doubted it, but anything could happen. That was just the way of life. You can plan all you want, but nothing ever goes a hundred percent, right?

DJ looked around to make sure no one else was near and that the couple was not in their living room before he came out of the woods. He looked through the living room sliding door glass window to make sure neither one of them came out of the back room and caught him. Back and forth, he scanned the area and then dashed out of the woods, jumping over the couple's railing and landing on their balcony.

"I guess they back there getting their groove on," DJ mumbled as he climbed up onto the railing, using the wall for support. The whole thing was awkward with the pump in DJ's hand, but he still was able to stand straight up. The railings didn't go all the way down. There was a space between the base of the balcony and the railing. Now he could slide the pump under it before pulling himself up to the second-floor balcony. He once again looked around to make sure nobody saw him. DJ had to be extra careful. He never knew when or if somebody could just so happen to be walking through the woods or somebody just happened to be sneaking out of their house and jumping over their railing while at the same time, he was jumping over a railing to break into somebody's house.

Once he knew everything was clear, he turned around to see how he would break into the sliding door without making too much noise. As he examined the door, he noticed it was already slightly ajar.

"Shit!" he cursed as he ducked down and put his ear to the door, trying to listen for any movement or sound inside the apartment.

"Damn! Don't nobody supposed to be here. This is supposed to be an easy lick. Man, I hope I don't have to smoke nobody ass tonight," DJ thought as he eased the door open a little. He thought this could be a setup, but why would Jessie set him up? He always played fair with Old Head Jessie, but it didn't stop Jessie the first time.

DJ had met Old Head Jessie a lil more than a year before he went to the pen. Back then, DJ was young, dumb, and didn't care about anything or nobody in the streets. He would run around and shoot people just because he could, loving the power the cold sense gave him until one day, Old Head Jessie pulled him to the side and changed everything.

"Come and take a walk with me." He told DJ as he approached him.

"For what?" DJ asked.

"I wanna show you something. You can trust me, Young Buck. I'm not even strapped, so you have the upper hand," Jessie said as he raised his shirt to show DJ that he didn't have a pistol. DJ reached under his shirt, gripping the gun he had tucked in the waist of his pants, hesitantly followed Jessie. Jessie stopped at the trunk of a beat-up BMW, looked back at DJ, gave him a stern look, and opened the trunk.

DJ's eyes damn near popped out of his head when he saw the two dead bodies in the car's trunk. The bodies weren't DJ's problem, as he already had a few of his own. It seems that professionals killed the two dead men in the trunk, judging by how Jessie killed them. The men were both hog-tied. Their throats were slit with burn marks all over their bodies from being tortured with some form of fire.

"Why are you showing me this?" DJ asked.

Instead of answering, Jessie went to the driver's side of the car and pulled out a duffel bag. That was the first time DJ ever saw two hundred grand, up close and in person, but it surely wasn't going to be his last.

"Listen, Young Buck," Jessie began, "If you're gonna be running around here shooting people and causing havoc, get some money out of it. I can teach you how to be a pro at robbing big-time drug dealers and how to put a nigga to sleep without always having to shoot him."

"Son, if you keep running around here the way you are, somebody will either put you in the dirt or snitch on you to get you off the radar because they're scared of you. Give it a few days to let it run through your mind, then get back at me. You should know how to find me."

"I don't need to think about it," young DJ told him. "I'm trying to learn what I have to so I can get paid. What do I have to do?"

Back then, DJ was only sixteen years old, going on seventeen years old and Jessie taught him almost everything you could name, from kidnapping to breaking into houses to killing and leaving no trace. They were like ghosts, and DJ loved every minute of it, so he couldn't figure out why Jessie would cross him. DJ hoped this wasn't a setup, or he'll have to kill Jessie this time.

"Well, I'm not going to find out standing out here."

Slowly he slid the screen door open more, then the glass sliding door. He waited a few seconds to see if any shadows had moved. He crawled in, gun first, in case someone did jump out at him. He peeked around the first wall on his right, looking down the hallway, then around the next wall to his right but a little further into the kitchen. Scooting backward with his gun pointed towards the hallway, he checked to see if the couple had locked the deadbolt on the front door before putting the chain lock on it. Slowly, he crawled down the hallway stopping at the first room on his right. The door was partially opened, allowing a soft melody to escape from inside that you couldn't hear until you got close to it. Before entering the room, he quietly checked the bathroom on his left and then the master bedroom at the end of the hall.

DJ could smell the sex before entering the room behind a teenage boy pumping like a jackhammer. The boy was so focused on what he was doing that he never even noticed DJ stand up behind him. DJ smiled as he looked at the boy humping with his pants down around his ankles. Pulling out his revolver, DJ whispered into the boy's ear.

"I guess you can say you got caught with your pants down, huh? Move again, and I'll blow your balls into her!"

DJ rested the gun barrel in between the boy's butt cheeks. His whole body stiffened as he tried to squeeze his butt cheeks close to remove the cold steel from between them.

"Danny, why did you stop, baby?" The girl whined, sitting up in the bed.

"Th---there's a man standing behind me, Renee, with a gun in...in my ass!" Danny stated stuttering.

"What? What do you mean there is---"

"Bitch, you heard what he said. Now shut the fuck up unless you tryna meet your maker before you're supposed to!" DJ blurted out, stepping from behind Danny so Renee could see him. DJ took another step back from Danny and switched hands holding the gun so he could pick up the pump shotgun from the floor.

"A'ight, now that I have both of y'all's full attention, let's get down to business but first, let me lay down the ground rules. Actually, there's only one rule. Do something stupid, and Im'ma kill you. Do as I say, and nobody will be hurt."

"Are you sure?" The girl asked, frightened, sounding much younger than she should have been.

"You have my word. Now, who da fuck are y'all?" DJ asked.

"I'm Neka. I live here, and that's my boyfriend, Danny."

WHACK! WHACK!

DJ smacked Danny across the head with the butt of the gun, knocking him down.

"Damn, I have to stop doing that, or Im'ma give somebody brain damage one day," DJ said, talking to himself.

"Why did you do that?" Neka screamed out. "Why?!

"Because I don't need him. Now, who are you to Big Tony?"

"That's my daddy!" Neka answered, rolling her eyes.

"So, you're Big Tony's daughter, huh?" DJ said, making it more of a statement than a question the way he intended it to be.

"So, where does daddy keep his money?"

"You're here to rob us?" Neka asked, surprised.

"Why the hell did you think I was here? I know you didn't think I came to see 'ya little freak show?"

"Can I put my clothes on?" Neka asked, with her arms folded across her chest, trying to conceal her breast.

"Yeah, go ahead!" DJ replied, ready to tell her no but changed his mind as he glanced into her young teenage face. She couldn't be over fifteen years old, DJ thought while allowing her to put her clothes on.

"You're gonna show me where your daddy keeps his stash after you get dressed."

"We don't have any money!" Neka yelled, putting on her clothes.

"Correction! You don't have any money, but Big Tony does, which belongs to me now."

"Y'all niggas always wanna rob somebody!" Neka snapped, disregarding the gun following her every movement. She continued yelling and rolling her neck around so hard that DJ thought her head would fall off and roll against the wall. But he tried to help her out a little, being the nice guy he was. DJ pulled back his right hand... then *SMACK*! He struck her in the face knocking her across the bed. Then he walked around the bed, forcefully picked Neka up by her throat, and choke slammed her onto the bed.

"No! No! Please!" Neka begged as blood began seeping through the side of her lips. DJ then ripped her clothes back off, laughing at Neka as she begged and tried fighting him, thinking he was trying to rape her.

DJ yanked her up by the hair, dragging her across the bed. He then flung her onto the floor, landing on top of Danny.

"Bitch, stop moving before I put a hole in both of y'all's heads! I tried to be nice, but naw you had to keep running your trap. Now I'm gonna leave y'all here for Big Tony to find. I wonder what he's going to say about his teenage daughter in here fucking while he's in the streets."

Instantly, Neka rolled over onto her stomach, moaning and grabbing her head. DJ rolled Danny on top of her and started duct taping them together first round the waist, then the ankles, and then their necks. DJ then smacked Neka across the head with his gun sending her into a daze.

Once he finished, he dragged them both into the middle of the living room for Big Tony to see as soon as he walked through the front door.

DJ went room to room, ram sacking the apartment looking for money and drugs before finally finding a safe in the bathroom closet.

"Shit!" DJ mumbled. "Now, Im'ma have to wait for the nigga to come home." He couldn't help but laugh, thinking, "I guess Jessie didn't show me everything because I damn sure can't open up no safe."

He knew he didn't have time to keep waiting for Big Tony, so he searched for another stash. A true hustle wouldn't keep all their chips in one spot for times like this.

"Jack Pot!" DJ exclaimed, finding a trash bag full of money under the kitchen sink.

"Im'ma have to settle for this right now but tell daddy I will be back for the rest," DJ stated to Neka as he entered the living room with the bag of money.

He didn't want to take the chance of the guy in the car's trunk waking up and somebody calling the cops, so he settled with what he got. A lil something is better than nothing. At least he didn't leave empty handed.

"Oh yeah," he said to Neka. SMACK! He delivered a powerful blow across her head with the butt of the gun, knocking her out.

"Damn, I love doing that!" He said, walking out of the front door.

Chapter 9
DANA

Dana woke up the following day to find DJ asleep in the chair beside her bed.

"What's he doing here?" Dana wondered. She knew he wasn't there when she fell asleep, which was late, so he had to come in sometime early in the morning.

"Well, at least I know he's not here to kill me because if he was, he wouldn't be asleep."

"Damn, I need answers, and the man who has them, the man I fell asleep thinking about, is sitting right beside me, and I don't even know what to say," she thought.

"Do you always stare at people while they're sleeping?" DJ asked. Dana was so into her thoughts she hadn't even realized DJ had opened his eyes.

"Nooo, I was just trying to figure out what you're doing here, and when did you get here?"

"Well, I can't even tell you what time I got here, but I came to make sure that you were alright."

"What do you mean to make sure I'm alright? Ain't nobody gonna do shit to me," Dana said, getting hyped up.

"Yo, chill! Calm down, lil momma. You realize that you got shot and are in the hospital, right? Nobody is talking about doing anything to you. At least, I hope not. All I was trying to say is I came to be by your side, and I refuse to let anything happen to you if I can help it."

"Now I know you've been trying to get with me for a while and...,"

"Hold up nigga! What? You're tryna to play me talking 'bout I've been trying to get with you for a while. Nigga, you got me twisted fo'real!" Dana butted in, cutting DJ off in mid-sentence.

"Dana! Are you going to let me talk, or are you gonna keep acting crazy, cutting me off?"

"Ok, ok, my bad. Go ahead and talk. I just hope that you're getting somewhere with this." Dana enjoyed pushing DJ almost to the limit, playing a little cat and mouse games with him, but she knew not to push him too far or else he wouldn't finish what he was saying, which she really wanted him to do.

"Like I was saying before I was so rudely interrupted. I know that you have been trying to get 'wit me for a while and believe me, I feel the same way as you do. But do you think you can deal 'wit a nigga like me?"

"DJ, I know what you do out there in those streets, and I don't care because I know you do what you have to for your family and the people you consider family."

"DJ, you have a good heart, and that's what I love about you. I don't understand you, though. If you feel me the way you say you do, why didn't you ever write back to me when you were in prison? I know most guys in prison would give anything to have a beautiful woman to ride with them, but it seemed like it didn't matter to you."

"Oh, believe me, it matters. I didn't want to get used to you writing and coming to see me, then one day it all stops."

DJ...Out for Blood

"Come on now, DJ. You should know that I wouldn't have done you like that!"

"Dana, you can't say what would or wouldn't have happened, but fuck all that. That's the past. It's about here and now. I almost lost you, and that shit made me open my eyes. You're going home with me when you get discharged from here."

"Alright, DJ," was all Dana could say. She'd been waiting for this moment for a long time and knew that DJ meant every word he said, or else he wouldn't have said it. He wasn't the type to say he would do something, then don't. If he said it, he meant it.

Chapter 10
DJ

"*Damn*," DJ thought. Speaking his mind to Dana felt like it was the hardest thing DJ had ever done. He wasn't good with talking about the way he felt or anything else about him, for that matter. If she had kept cutting him off, he wouldn't have finished what he was trying to say and needed to get his thoughts out right then and there.

DJ remained at the hospital, spending time with Dana until the six o'clock news came on. The headlines read:

MAN FOUND IN TRUNK OF CAR
ON RICHMOND'S SOUTH SIDE

He let the guy that he carjacked live since there was no reason to kill him. When he left Big Tony's apartment, he didn't go back to the car. He went and hotwired another one. There was no reason to ride extra, especially with the white guy in the trunk and all the money he had quickly acquired.

"You good nigga? You're really in deep thought over there.

They sat in the car, watching Dana's house to see who came and went. DJ slowly opened his eyes and looked over at Trill. He didn't tell her he thought her best friend tried to set him up because, to be truthful, DJ wasn't even sure yet if she did, but he was going to find out by the end of the night. Before leaving the hospital, he took Dana's house keys and the ones to her car.

He planned on painting her car, using it as a low-key car for him, and buying her something new that he would surprise her with once she

58

got out of the hospital.

He took the house keys so he could walk straight into Dana's house and catch Tracy off guard. He wanted to see how she would react to seeing him, and if it wasn't the way he wanted it to be, he would kill her on the spot.

"Yeah, I'm good, dawg. Just thinking about how Tracy and Dana are best friends, it will kill her if Tracy ends up dead."

No sooner than those words left DJ's lips, his cell phone started ringing.

"Damn dawg. Dana is calling now." DJ smiled as his phone lit up with the hospital number displayed across the screen.

"She must feel her nigga thinking about her."

"Nigga, you crazy! That girl got you bugged. Don't you think it's crazy that she called soon as you said something about killing Tracy?" Trill asked.

"Nigga, stop trippin'!" DJ said as he pressed the send button.

"What's up, baby?" he asked, answering the phone.

"DJ, we need to talk. Now!" Dana hollered out.

"Alright, what's wrong? Can it wait till later?"

"No, DJ. It can't! I know what you're ready to do!"

"Dana, what are you talking about?" DJ asked.

"You're going after Tracy! DJ, I'm not as stupid as you think I am." DJ didn't know what to say after hearing what Dana said. He looked over at Trill, thinking maybe she does have me bugged.

B. MILLER

TRACY

Tracy almost pissed on herself when she looked out the window and noticed DJ and Trill sitting in front of Dana's house. If they had been in any other car besides one of Trill's decked-out cars, she wouldn't have noticed them but being that they were, she did because she knew every car he drove.

She knew DJ would think she had a part in the shooting at the club if he remembered seeing her that night with Tee.

"Shit!" Tracy yelled out. "I didn't even have anything to do with the shooting DJ. You should know I will never put Dana in harm's way, and I'm not stupid enough to set your mentally challenged ass up!" She yelled, talking to DJ as if he could hear her.

"I know Dana is most likely mad with me for not being there with her, but she's going to have to understand my reason for not being there and try to talk some sense in her nut case friend."

"Matter of fact, where's my phone?"

"Hello! Dana! It's me, Tracy."

DJ...Out for Blood

DANA

When DJ left the hospital, Dana was again left alone, back to her thoughts. She knew DJ planned on catching Tracy at some point in time. That's why he asked for the keys to her house. Everybody knew that's where she stayed most of the time.

Dana didn't know that DJ was going straight over there when he left the hospital. She thought she would have a few days to talk with him about Tracy before he did anything to her.

"I wonder why he didn't tell me he was going around there right now. His ass knew he was going," Dana said, pondering.

"I'm not as stupid as DJ thinks I am. I know his ass also had something to do with that guy being found in the trunk of that car. Soon as it came on the news, he got all quiet and very interested in it, then he left. But DJ didn't see the part where they found two people tied up in the same apartment complex the white guy in the trunk was located. The only difference was that the couple was found inside the apartment.

Not even an hour after DJ left, Tracy called, saying that DJ was there to kill her. Dana had to get her to calm down before she could fully understand what she was saying.

"How do you know he's there to kill you?" Dana asked. Before getting hysterical again, Tracy told her that DJ and Trill were sitting outside the house watching everybody and had been out there for at least ten minutes.

Tracy was so scared. Dana didn't bother asking why she never came to the hospital or even called to check on her. Dana decided to let it slide for a while until she found a way to get DJ and Trill to back off her.

DJ was the key. She knew Trill would follow if she could get DJ to fall back. But the question is, how does she supposed to get DJ to fall back?

"Fuck it! Im'ma just call him!"

DJ...Out for Blood

DJ

"Dana! What the hell are you talking about? That medication got you trippin' fo'real," DJ stated before covering the mouthpiece on the phone to whisper to Trill what she had just said.

While laughing, Trill yelled back a little too loud. "Nigga, I told your simple ass she got you bugged."

"Dawg, that shit ain't funny! This is her best friend that I'm thinking about killing, and you over here laughing," DJ whispered.

"DJ, I know you are sitting in front of my house with Trill, and I know y'all have been out there for almost fifteen minutes now."

"Dana, stop trippin'!" DJ said, starting to get frustrated.

"Damn, DJ! Stop lying and keep it real!"

"Nobody's lying, Dana."

"So, y'all are not outside of my house?"

"No."

"So, who is sitting outside my house in the same all-black Cutlass that Trill drives? Especially when he's trying to be low-key?"

"Who the fuck is this?" DJ asked.

"This is Tracy, DJ, and I'm looking out the window at y'all watching me watch y'all asses! I know every car that Trill drives," Tracy said.

DJ looked over to Trill, giving him the evil eye and letting him know they had to talk later.

"Alright, so what if I am in front of the house? That don't mean I'm after you." There was dead silence.

"What? You in there feeling guilty or something, Tracy?"

Trill looked at DJ wide-eyed when he heard him say Tracy's name. DJ put his finger to his lips, indicating for him to be quiet.

"No, I'm not feeling guilty! It's not even what you think, DJ?"

"How do you know what I'm thinking?"

"DJ, everybody knows how you are when you're mad. If you even thin—"

"Look, Tracy!" DJ said, cutting her off in mid-sentence before she said something crazy over the phone. "Come outside so we can talk. You have my word that nothing's gonna happen to you.

"DJ, I say this in no disrespectful way, but I don't trust you when you're mad."

"I'm not mad," DJ said, trying to sound calm.

"How about everybody just meet at the hospital?" Dana said, breaking into the conversation.

"Tracy, you haven't been here to see me yet, so this will be a good time to come and explain yourself."

"Dana, you, of all people, should know it's not like that."

"I do, but I still wanna hear your reasons for not being here by my side. So, what's it gonna be?"

"Soon as Trill and DJ pull off, I'm on my way."

"A'ight, we're leaving now. Pull off Trill," DJ barked out.

After he told Dana he would see her in a few minutes, he hung up and turned his attention to Trill.

"Man, how the fuck are you gonna drive a car over there that Tracy knows? What if she had called the cops instead of Dana? We would have either had to shoot it out with them or go to jail without bail. And I'm not going back to jail!"

"DJ, my bad, dawg. I didn't think she would remember this car because she only saw it about a year ago."

"It's all good. We're still free, but you must remember that women have a photographic memory and be more careful when we're doing dirt here."

"If she digs you as you told me she does, then she's gonna try to remember every little thing about you. Shit that you don't even know that she knows."

Even though DJ had to school Trill from time to time, he stayed calm about it. He knew that getting mad wasn't gonna help any. He was just glad that she called Dana and not the law. If the cops had shown up, it would have been a problem. He meant he wasn't going back to jail. That wasn't even an option.

DANA

Dana couldn't understand how or why, but Tracy arrived at the hospital first. She left the house ten minutes after DJ and Trill, keeping Dana on the phone until she walked into the hospital's front door. She didn't believe that DJ would leave like he said he would; to be honest, Dana didn't either but hoped he had. There was no telling with DJ. He was unpredictable.

"Dana, you have to believe me. I didn't have anything to do with the shooting," Tracy said, trying to explain herself to Dana, even though Dana did believe her.

"Tracy, you haven't given me a reason to believe you yet," Dana responded. "I mean, I have been here for over a week, and now you're just coming to see me? This is the only reason you needed me to get DJ off your back."

"Sis, I did try to come to see you. The first time I came, I saw DJ walking to the elevator, so I turned around and left. Dana, I was scared; truth be told, I'm still scared. Every time I tried to see you, DJ was here, and far as I can tell, he hasn't left your side."

Dana smiled, hearing Tracy say DJ stayed by her side. When she came out of her coma, DJ was the first face she saw, and now every time Dana goes to sleep, she hopes he's there when she wakes up.

"Tracy, why didn't you try to talk to DJ?" Dana asked, already knowing the answer.

"Dana, you already know there is no talking to DJ when he's mad, and Trill act just like him…fucking DJ Junior," Tracy teased.

DJ...Out for Blood

"Well, DJ did raise Trill," Dana said.

"Shit, right after you got shot, somebody killed Tee, his son, his son's mother, and Tee's boy. After they killed them, they set the house on fire. That shit had DJ and Trill's names written all over it, and you wanna know why I didn't try to talk to that nut case? Girl, be real!"

"Tracy, I do believe you. I just had to make you sweat a little," Dana said, trying not to laugh at how Tracy talked about DJ and Trill. They are nut cases but only to those who cross them.

"Alright, answer this for me. Why didn't you call me?"

"Giiiirl, didn't I just say you had the damn terminator sitting up in this bitch with you!"

"Ok, Ok. I got you!" Dana said. "I wonder where they're at anyways. They should've been here by now."

"They're probably out killing somebody," Tracy said, getting hyped up.

"Girl, sit your simple ass down before somebody hears you."

"Someone needs to talk to them, Dana fo'real! Fucking Doc Holiday and Billy the Kid! They can't keep going around killing people, or somebody will snitch on them, and I don't want either of them to go to jail."

"Shit, me either! DJ just came home, and he's finally mine. I can't lose him when I just got him. So, how do we talk to them?" Dana asked, starting to tear up.

Tracy had just made Dana realize she might lose DJ to jail again, and she'll be damn if she was gonna let that happen again, so they had to figure out something.

"Well, word on the streets is that DJ's going to kill everybody that runs with Big Tony's team because they knew Tee was at him, and you got shot instead."

"Tracy, stop lying!" Dana exclaimed, knowing she had to be twisting the story like she always does.

"Girl, I'm not playing. Word is Doc Holiday then lost a few more of his marbles over you getting shot, so you need to be the one to talk to him."

"Well, I have to find him first. They should've been here by now."

"Yeah, they should have been. I left the house after they did. Girl, soon as I saw them pull off, I dashed out the door. Shit, I wasn't even going to give them fools a chance to come back walking."

"Tracy, your ass is crazy! Do you really think Trill will do anything to you?"

"To be honest, I don't even know. We've been messing around with each other off and on for a while now. At one time, I wasn't worried about Trill hurting me, but now that your psycho man is home, I'm having second thoughts."

"We just have to let DJ know what actually happened," Dana said, trying to keep Tracy calm because she was starting to look scared again.

"Matter of fact, hand me the phone, so I can see why they're not here yet, and they better have a damn good reason."

DJ...Out for Blood

DJ

"Y'all dumb fucks breaks into my crib, duct tapes my daughter, and then steals my stash? Y'all got the game fucked up fo'real!" Big Tony yelled.

"Nigga! You better wake up and realize where the fuck you're at before you get your dumb ass bodied out here."

Big Tony didn't exactly know where DJ lived. So, he went to the park adjacent to his house, which would prove to be a big mistake. DJ's crew of young bucks were in full battle mode. They loved shooting people just because of the thrill.

On the way to the hospital, DJ lil homie Vell called his phone, letting him know Big Tony was running his mouth. DJ smiled and told Vell to fall back and not do anything until he arrived.

When DJ and Trill walked into the park, Vell and Big Tony were going at it. Little did Big Tony know that Vell was the worst one of his young bucks to go into a verbal battle with. Big Tony would have been dead if it wasn't for DJ telling Vell to chill until he got there.

"Lil Tony, you need to calm the fuck down or get laid the fuck down!" DJ tried to be funny by calling Tony "lil" as he and Trill walked up.

"Fuck you DJ! What? You think you're bulletproof or something? Well, guess what? You're not nigga! You bleed just like us. Remember that!"

"Tony, I'm not gonna tell you again," DJ said calmly.

"Nigga fuck..."

"Vell!" DJ shouted.

POW! POW!

Big Tony didn't even get the "you" out of his mouth before Vell shot him two times in the head.

DJ began patting himself down, trying to figure out why his body was vibrating. Going over his pockets, he realized it was his cell phone ringing.

"What's up? He asked, answering the phone, relieved that a bullet didn't strike him as he thought.

"DJ, where are y'all at? We have been waiting for half an hour now! Are y'all coming to the hospital or what?" Dana asked on the other end of the phone.

"Dana, hold on for a second!" DJ said before pressing the MUTE button. "What did you say, Vell?"

"I said, what do you wanna do about these two clowns that came with Fat Tony?"

DJ looked over to where Fat Tony boys were standing off to their side.

"Damn fools!" DJ thought. "They should have at least tried to run."

"Kill 'em," DJ said in one breath and walked off.

DJ unmuted the phone. "Yeah, I'm back, baby!" He spoke into the phone.

"Sooo...?"

"So what?" DJ asked.

"Are you still coming to the hospital or not?" Dana asked .

"Yeah."

POW! POW! POW!

"Look, we're on the way now!"

"What the hell was that noise, DJ?"

"Trill, let's roll," DJ said, hanging up the phone without answering Dana.

"A yo Vell! Im'ma get 'wit you later and hit you up my nigga. Y'all go and lay low for a while. You know them people are gonna be out here in a minute.

"That's what's up, Big homie!" Vell said, walking off.

DJ and Trill got into the car and pulled off with DJ in thinking mode.

"Damn, now I'm not gonna get the rest of Big Tony's stash."

DANA

"Girl, I think you were right! I think they just shot somebody!"

"Why in the hell you say that Dana? I was just joking!"

"Well, I'm not!" Dana yelled louder than she intended to. She told Tracy how DJ had told her to hold on, and he forgot what they were talking about to her hearing gunshots in the background and DJ hanging up on her.

"Dana, are you sure?" Tracy asked.

"Hell yeah, I'm sure! I know what gunshots sound like, and I heard about five or six shots in DJ's background." Just as the words left Dana's mouth, Trill walked into the room without DJ. Dana's heart started racing, thinking that DJ didn't come. Before she could ask Trill where he was, he walked in with a giant teddy bear and some roses.

"Hey, baby! He said, walking over to kiss Dana.

"I hope you like the stuff I brought you!" he said.

"I told that nigga don't get that shit!" Trill blurted out.

"Shut up, Trill! Ain't nobody ask you," Tracy said, rolling her eyes.

"Thank you, baby!" Dana said, trying to sound sweet.

"Can you sit it on the table for me, please?"

"Listen, DJ and Trill. We need to talk," Dana said, taking a deep breath before proceeding.

"Awww shit, here we go. Man, I hate when women start that we need to talk mess," Trill said starting to pace the floor. "I hate talking. What's there to talk about anyway?"

"Boy, just sit your retarded ass down and listen!" Tracy said, now rolling her head around on her neck.

"Yeah, we do need to talk," DJ said, looking directly at Tracy.

DJ

"DJ, why are you looking at me like that?" Tracy asked, scared to roll her head around as she did with Trill.

"Tracy, stop playing games with me. You already know what's the deal."

"What is it that you want to know, DJ?"

"So, you're just gonna keep playing stupid, huh? Alright, fuck it! Explain why you was pointing at me and Dana at the club when you were with Tee?"

"So, you do think that I tried to set you up?"

"Look, just answer the damn question, Tracy!" DJ said, starting to get agitated with all the games Tracy was playing.

"Calm down my nigga!" Trill said, speaking up for Tracy and pulling her towards him.

"What the fuck!" DJ thought. That was the first time Trill had shown him any emotion towards a female. I wonder why he never told me that he felt something for her. If he had, this wouldn't have even went this far. That's a'ight. I'll ask him later. Naw, fuck that! I have to ask him now.

"So, what, you got some type of feelings for her?" DJ asked.

"DJ!" Dana called out to him trying to get him to ease up but DJ wasn't leaving it alone. He had to find out.

"Dana, stay out of this!" Trill was quiet for a moment, then hesitantly nodded his head yes.

"Damn it, Trill! Why didn't you even tell me?" DJ asked. "You're supposed to tell me shit like that."

"Shit, you!?" Tracy said, wiping her eyes. "This is news to me!"

"DJ, you know how you get sometimes. I don't know whether I should or shouldn't show any kind of emotions around you."

"Come on, Trill. You're like a lil brother to me. You know that you can tell me anything, even if it's gonna make me mad. If you had told me you felt something for Tracy, we could have gone about this another way."

"So, y'all was there to kill me!" Tracy yelled out.

"Nigga, get off of me!" she said, pushing Trill away.

"Well, yeah, and naw," DJ answered.

"That's not a damn answer, DJ. Which one is it?" Tracy said, putting her hands on her hips and rolling her head around like a bobblehead doll.

"Look, Tracy!" DJ started. "We came to give you a chance to explain yourself."

"Trill!" Tracy called out, looking over to him to defend her.

"He's telling the truth, Tracy," Trill said. "But if you were lying, we would've had no choice but to kill you."

"And you were gonna help him?" Tracy asked with a wide eye.

"I don't have a choice. DJ raised me like I was his son. He told me I didn't have to hustle and would make sure I was good long as I stayed in school and got good grades. If it wasn't for him, I wouldn't be who I am today."

"Tracy, I care about you. I really do, but if you tried to set up DJ and I had to choose sides, it would be him just like DJ will take my side over Dana."

"DJ!" Dana said, butting in, looking from Trill to DJ. "You'll choose Trill over me if it came down to it?"

"Yeah, I would," replied DJ. "I will never let anybody or anything come between us if I can help it."

"Tee wanted to know where Dana was at, so I pointed in y'all direction, telling him she was here with her boo, so he had to find somebody else to try and holla at."

"DJ, I never tried to set you up. Dana is my best friend, DJ, and the only family I have left out here, and I will never, I mean never in my life, put her in harm's way. I also know how much she cares about you, and it will hurt her if something happens to you, so I will never try to put you in harm's way. Plus, your ass is crazy. I don't have time to be messing around with you."

"Now, was that so hard to say?" Goes DJ. "That's all I wanted to know."

"Anyway, listen, me and Trill have some business that we need to tend to, so we're going to have to cut this short."

"Y'all have to stop killing people," Dana said softly.

Trill looked at DJ then they both looked over at Dana. DJ didn't know what to say because he knew Dana didn't know about Tee and his family. How could she? She had been in a coma then, but motor mouth Tracy wasn't, and he knew she heard about them.

"What are you talking about now, Dana?" DJ asked.

DJ...Out for Blood

"DJ, when the news came on about that man being found in the trunk of his car, you got all quiet and real interested like you knew about what happened, then you quickly left. Soon as you walked out of the room, they showed two more people duct-taped around the same apartment complex, and I know that lil girl is Big Tony's daughter."

"Why does it have to be me that done it?" DJ inquired.

"Because everybody knows your M.O. baby. So, all of that heat is going to point at both of you because they know y'all roll together."

"Also, y'all," Tracy cut in, "the word on the streets is that y'all supposed to get at everybody that rides with Tee and Big Tony."

An alarm went off in DJ's head when Tracy said everybody on Tee's and Big Tony's team. He had only told that to one person and it damn sure wasn't Trill. He had only told Trill they were gonna get at everybody involved, not the whole team. Trill had just found out about him running up in Big Tony's spot on the ride to the hospital. Yeah, it was time for him to chill out until he dealt with the snitch,

"Alright, me and Trill are gonna go lay low for a while and try to keep our hands clean," DJ said, not knowing what else to tell the women. He wasn't about to admit anything to them, so he let them think what they wanted, and he still wasn't calling off what he had planned for the night.

Chapter 11
DJ

"Bra, your ass is crazy!" Trill said, laughing. "I could've sworn you said we were gonna lay low for a while?"

"We are my nigga. Just not today. I told the women what they wanted to hear to keep them calm. We'll start laying low after tonight," DJ replied.

Not even an hour later after then he told Dana and Tracy that he and Trill were going to lay low, they were sitting in front of Big Tony's parent's house in Henrico County. They had to be extra careful out in that neighborhood because sitting outside in the car could make someone suspicious enough to call the cops.

"So, what's the plan?" Trill asked.

"Shit, this one is really simple, my nigga. We let the house fill up with Big Tony's family, then we run up and swiss cheese the entire house. Whoever gets it, gets it and whoever doesn't, doesn't," DJ answered.

"Hold up, DJ! I have never questioned your judgment, but what's the point of all of this?" Trill was curious. "I mean, you always taught me that if it's not about money or family, then it's not worth it. We already killed Tee, Vell killed Big Tony, and the rest of their crew don't matter because without them shit is dead."

"And you're right, but we're doing this to send a message to those few niggas in Big Tony's crew that might wanna try their hand that we are not to be fucked with. Also, by doing this, we can draw some of the heat away from us. Everybody knows that we kidnap and do everything professional for money, not run around and shoot up houses as lil niggas do."

"Tru, tru. I'm feeling that!" said Trill. "I just hope everything goes as planned."

"Yeah, me too, but you know as well as I do that most of the time, nothing ever goes as planned. If something goes sideways, we go back to the spot and shoot anyone who tries to stop us."

DJ and Trill were strapped with AR-15 assault rifles with one hundred round magazines on them, plus two backup pistols a piece.

"Let's roll!" DJ said, exiting the car.

They ran to a side window with a full view of everybody in the living room. Since the house was so small, DJ figured they probably had a full view of everyone in the house. The house was one level with two bedrooms, one bathroom, a kitchen, and a living room that was half the dining room. They could see the entire living and dining room, half of the kitchen, and straight down the short hallway from where they were standing. Big Tony's family and friends were roaming around the house hugging and trying to comfort one another when DJ asked Trill if he was ready. Trill answered by cocking the AR and pointing it at the house. DJ did the same.

"NOW!" DJ yelled as he opened fire.

Chop! Chop! Chop! Chop! Chop! Chop!

DJ started backing up towards the car with Trill following suit, then stopped shooting to jump into the car and putting it in drive. They had left the car running so they could make a fast getaway. Soon as the car began rolling forward, DJ stopped shooting and jumped in. Trill pulled off like nothing ever happened to keep from drawing too much attention to the car.

Trill drove down a side street for almost two blocks before turning off onto Azalea Avenue, the main street. Cop cars were coming towards them fast. Red, white, and blue lights were flashing, sirens blazing. DJ just hoped they didn't try to pull them over. DJ was calm on the outside, but on the inside, his heart was racing a hundred miles per second. He looked over at Trill, who was also calm, but DJ could tell he was also nervous. Their adrenaline was pumping, hoping the police didn't make a U-turn and follow them but prepare for if they did. They cruised for a few blocks, watching the cop cars fade through the rearview mirror before Trill turned onto Old Brook Road into the city.

"We should be good now, Bra. You know Henrico police don't usually cross the county limit line into the city," Trill said.

All DJ could think was, *"Yeah, usually."*

DJ...Out for Blood

DANA

Once again, Dana was left alone with her thoughts. Tracy had already left long ago after DJ and Trill, saying she'll be back tomorrow. Dana sat in the room pouting while she flicked through the channels on the TV, mad that she couldn't get in touch with DJ and that nothing was on TV but the news.

She'd been trying to call him for the past hour only to get his voice mail every time.

"Damn! I hope he's not out there doing nothing stupid after the talk we just had. That would just be plain old dumb." Dana mumbled.

"Shit, let me turn this up!" Dana said, talking to herself. The BREAKING NEWS headline on her TV caught her attention.

"Four people wounded, two dead, and at least a dozen in shock over a shooting that just occurred." The anchorman continued.

"A man known as Richmond City's Big Tony was killed earlier today, and his family was having a family dinner to mourn his death when someone opened fire on the house. The police have no motive for the shooting as of this moment or suspects, but they found numerous spent rifle shell casings outside the house. Detectives also say the shooting might also be connected to the killing of Big Tony."

"If anyone has any information, please contact crime stoppers at the number listed on the TV screen."

"I'm so glad you just saw that. Now I won't have to explain why I'm here!" Dana looked over in the direction of where the voice was coming from. Standing by the room's door was the same detective she had the nurse put out, only he was by himself this time.

"I wonder what he meant by saying he's glad I saw what the news just said?" Dana thought.

"What do you want now?" Dana snapped.

"Look, Ms. Davis. The last time I was here, we got off on a bad start so let's start over."

"I guess he's supposed to be the good cop this time. I hope he knows I'm not saying shit!" Dana thought to herself.

"Ms. Davis, I'm Detective Anderson, investigating the shooting you were involved in at the club. I need to know if you remember anything that happened that night?"

"No!" Dana shot out, looking him straight into the eyes.

"Well, let me ask you this, Ms. Davis. What is your relationship with Davon Jackson?"

"We're good friends!" Dana replied, rolling her eyes. "Why? What's it to you?"

"Look, Ms. Davis, I know that y'all are more than just friends, and I know that you know more than what you are telling me. Since you got shot and he came home, people have been killed left and right. So, you can either tell me what you know or go down with him as an accomplice because he's going down!"

Dana looked at the detective sideways.

"Are you finished yet?" Dana asked him, not being affected by none of the detective threats. She figured that if he had any evidence on DJ, he wouldn't be there questioning her, trying to fish for information.

DJ...Out for Blood

"You little black ..." the detective started but didn't finish.

"Naw, don't stop now!" said Dana. "Go ahead and finish what you were gonna say! You little black B-I-T-C-H! That's what you wanted to say, right?" She yelled the last part louder to make him even madder than he already was.

Before the detective could respond, the room door flew open smacking the wall with DJ walking in and Trill following behind him.

DJ

DJ and Trill had just stepped off the elevator on Dana's floor at the hospital when they heard her yelling at someone. DJ reached her room full force to find Detective Anderson apple red in the face, pointing his finger at her.

Detective Anderson was the one who arrested DJ for murder. Allegedly, he paid people to testify against him, which sent him to prison. He was outraged when DJ only received eight years because the charge was reduced to manslaughter and swore to get him again once he was released.

"Detective Anderson, I would strongly advise you to keep your finger to yourself if you wanna keep it!" DJ stated.

"You threatening me, boy?" said Detective Anderson. "You know I can lock your black ass up right now for that, right?"

"Come on now, Detective. You, of all people, know I don't make threats. Besides, you are alone and gonna need an army to take me up out of here today."

"You got it for today, Davon!" Detective Answer said not wanting any problems with DJ. "I will get you though. You and your lil protégé, so wait and see." With that being said, the detective stormed out of the room.

"Are you alright, baby?" DJ asked Dana.

"Yeah, I'm good," she answered back. "He didn't do anything but ask a lot of questions about you."

"What kind of questions?" DJ asked, sitting down in the chair beside the bed.

"He wanted to know who you were to me."

"And what did you tell him?"

"I told him we were good friends, and he just snapped out!"

"DJ, you know that cracker has it out for you," Trill said

"Yeah, I know, and now he has it out for you," DJ replied.

"Look, Trill, tomorrow go lay low with Tracy somewhere. As a matter of fact, if y'all feel up to it, go and see if y'all can find two nice houses out in the county. If you're feeling Tracy like you say, one of the houses is y'alls, and the other one is for Dana and me.'

"Word! That's what's up, Dawg! If you are good, Im'ma go ahead and bounce now," Trill said.

"A'ight look. Holla at me in about two days. Dana gets out of the hospital tomorrow, so Im'ma spend the day with her and the family."

"Well, look. I'm out!" Trill said, giving DJ some dap before he left.

Detective Anderson was a real asshole, and not only did DJ have him on his ass again, but Dana's and Trill's as well. Anderson would do anything to send DJ back to prison, even if it meant locking Dana up on a trumped-up charge so she could put it off on DJ or, better yet, step up and take it.

DJ had never thought about killing a police officer before, but it was time for him to start thinking about it or move somewhere out of state which was far away from his mind.

"Baby, how do you know I'm getting out of the hospital tomorrow? Dana asked curiously.

"I talked with your doctor earlier today. I'm ready for you to get the hell out of here! Oh, I meant what I said about you coming home with me. My mom found a new house out in Highland Springs, and I think my daughter will stay with her. You know how they are.

"Yeah, your mother has your daughter spoiled rotten," Dana replied, smiling.

"Anyway, go ahead and get some rest, baby, because you're going to need it for tomorrow," DJ said, needing some time to clear his head.

While Dana laid back and rested, DJ tried to figure out a way to kidnap detective Anderson. He knew who he needed to talk to about it, but he also knew he couldn't trust that person.

"Fuck it!" DJ thought to himself. "Im'ma find out the information that I need to know, then Im'ma smoke his ass too. Oh yeah, the heat is really gonna be on now! Detective Anderson don't know who he's fucking with, but Im'ma show his ass better than I can tell him...in due time. They fucked up by sending me to prison for a murder they know I didn't commit. Now they let me loose back onto these streets. Now the streets are mine and niggas can either get on board or get out the way. It's their choice but if they don't hurry up and choose one, Im'ma help them out. Believe that!"

Chapter 12
DJ

DJ had awoken the following day, reaching for a gun that wasn't there because he and Trill had gotten rid of all their dirty guns by ditching them into the James River the night before they went to the hospital.

"Damn! How could I slip like this?" DJ thought until he realized that he was still in the hospital and that Dana was the person standing before him talking with the doctors.

"Good morning, Baby! Did you sleep well? What's wrong?" Dana asked, noticing the strange look DJ had on his face.

"I'm good!" DJ answered back as the doctors left; he was awoken but focused.

"We tried not to disturb you because you were sleeping so peacefully. I even kissed you, and you still didn't move!"

"Yeah, I had to be tired," thought DJ. "That comes from running these streets, robbing, and killing niggas.

"A yo, how you gonna kiss me while I'm sleeping?"

"Like this!" Dana replied, walking over to DJ and giving him another kiss. DJ put his tongue deep into Dana's mouth, allowing his tongue to memorize it. He figured she must have been up for a while because she smelled like she had just taken a shower and her breath tasted like Colgate toothpaste compared to his morning breath. Instantly, DJ's manhood stood long and firm, just thinking about what he wanted to do to her.

"Hold on, baby!" DJ said that coming up for air, he had to stop himself before things went too far in the hospital. He had to be home for almost a month and still hadn't slept with anybody. Pussy was the last thing on his mind because money was first. He knew once he got his money up, pussy would follow.

"What's wrong, baby?" Dana asked.

"We have to chill out!" replied DJ, "I'm not tryna start nothing that we're not gonna finish right now."

"Who said we can't finish right now?" asked Dana. "Let me find out you're scared nigga!"

"What? You don't want this DJ?" Dana asked, dropping her hospital gown down to the floor, exposing her nakedness.

"Now, this is what I'm talking about!" DJ said, pulling her onto his lap. He kissed her deep and rough to let her know he was hungry. DJ picked Dana up, kissing her gently along the nape of her neck, then carrying her over to the bed, laying her on her stomach. She arched her plump ass into the air for DJ to take her from behind, but he had other plans. Taking two of his fingers, he slowly eased them inside of her warm, moist pussy.

"Damn, she's tight," DJ thought as he pulled his fingers out, smelling them to make sure everything smelled right, then tasted them. He eased the same two fingers back inside her but only halfway this time, opening her moist pussy lips and began tongue kissing them. A soft moan escaped from Dana's mouth with her eyes rolling into the back of her head, biting down on her bottom lip, trying as best she could to moan lightly.

"Oh, god, DJ! Fuck me! Fuck me now!" she begged and pleaded.

DJ got up, pulled his hard dick out, and rammed it into her.

"Ummm, Ahhhh!" Dana moaned out, clenching the sheets with her now-clenched fingers.

"Whose pussy is this?" DJ asked, smacking her on the ass.

"It...it...it's your Baby! It's all yours whenever you want it, baby!"

DJ loved hearing those words come out of her mouth; he meant he would take advantage of it every chance he got. DJ then pulled his hard dick out of her dripping wet pussy, flipped her over, and dove back inside of her pushing her legs back so far he thought one of them was going to break.

"I'm cumming, baby! Baby, I'm cumming! Cum with me, baby, cum inside this pussy, DJ!" Dana whined. She didn't have to tell him twice before he released a whole load inside her.

"Damn, we must've forgotten we were still in the hospital," DJ said while pulling up his pants, watching Dana just lay there trying to get herself together.

"On second thought...no, we didn't! We just didn't care!" DJ said, laughing.

"Damn, if she keeps shit like this up, she won't have to ever worry about me cheating," DJ thought.

"Dana, get your ass up before somebody walks in here!"

"Oh, so now you're worried about somebody coming in here?! You should have thought about that when you were all up inside of me." DJ smiled.

"Girl, get your retarded ass up! And what were the doctors talking about?"

"Oh, he just told me to finish getting my rest while my body heals up, and he gave me my release papers.

"So, you can leave?" DJ asked, shocked.

"Yeah, soon as I get dressed."

"Woman, your ass is crazy fo'real!" DJ said, laughing.

"Awww nigga, don't front like you don't like that shit! I did that for you because I want you to know I'm all for you, all about you, and will do anything for you."

"You're trying to make a nigga fall in love fo'real, huh?"

"That's the plan. Is that so bad?"

"Naw, I guess not. But are you sure you can deal 'wit a nigga like me?"

"Please nigga!" Dana started, "I've always dealt with you whether you knew it or not. I've been with you since day one."

That was true. Dana had always stood by him, but he didn't look at her the way he does now. Even when he was in prison, she was holding him down without him having to ask.

"Naw, baby. It's not," said DJ, "and believe me, I appreciate everything you have done for me. Now come on and let's get up out of here!"

Chapter 13
DANA

It's been a month since Dana walked out of the hospital and DJ kept his word on almost everything he said he would do. He bought them a house a block away from his mother's home so he could be close to her and his daughter. He also bought Trill and Tracy a place two houses down from theirs. As far as Dana knew, DJ and Trill stayed out of trouble as promised. She didn't hear about any more murders that might have involved them.

The problem was that they hardly ever came home. Tracy stayed with Dana most of the time, so neither would have to stay home alone. Out of the two weeks they have been living in the house, DJ might have stayed home approximately four days...give or take a few, and every time Dana tried to say something to him about it, he always responded the same adage, *"This shit ain't free!"* Dana had to admit the house they lived in was gorgeous. The house not only had four bedrooms with three and a half bathrooms, a walk-in kitchen pantry, dining room, and not to mention the one place she loved to sit and relax while drinking a glass of wine was the living room with the enormous two-way fireplace.

"Fuck that!" Dana sat thinking to herself. "I know his ass got money. Three days ago, I counted one hundred and twenty thousand dollars for him. Plus, if he didn't-why he keeps spoiling Trill when he's a grown-ass man and has his own money? But, no, DJ still tried to do everything for him. Tracy felt the same way as Dana. She was also tired of Trill running the streets and not coming home. Soon as they walked through the front door, they would let their men have it!

DJ...Out for Blood

DJ

DJ and Trill had been out getting money for the past few weeks, grinding hard. When DJ's mom moved, he kept the house because it was in the hood and let his lil homie, Vell, stay there. DJ and Trill still had the four bricks they took from Tee the night they robbed and killed him. DJ gave Vell half a brick for killing Big Tony for him and told Vell that he had to re-up from him or Trill. It wasn't that DJ was on some bully shit. He just wanted to keep the money in their crew. Most of the time, DJ and Trill were with Vell, trying to build up their team and money. He moved up fast in the game, selling weight, being that many of the young bucks looked up to him and bought coke from him. Vell even took notice of what they were trying to do, plucking off everybody who wasn't trying to move up in the game and plotting on everybody they didn't trust.

Without Trill and Vell, DJ would probably be sitting on the cake he had for about six months. They were the real keys to his operation. That's why he tried to do everything he could for them. He looked out for who looked out for him.

"These two niggas won't ever want for nothing as long as I'm around," DJ thought, looking at both Vell and Trill.

"Yo, let's go out tonight!" DJ said, taking another shot of gin. They were sitting on the porch drinking.

"I know Dana and Tracy wanna get out of the house. We've been keeping them in there like they're locked up."

"You know I'm 'wit it!" Vell said, hyped up.

"Nigga, you're 'wit anything!" Trill said, laughing, "but DJ, do you think Dana is ready to go back to the club yet? She hasn't been out since the night she got shot."

"Yeah, you're right, Dawg. Let me call and ask her," DJ replied.

"Ask Tracy too! I know her ass is over there," Trill said.

"A'ight."

DJ...Out for Blood

DANA

Dana and Tracy were sitting in the den talking about their men when the house phone rang, temporarily interrupting their conversation. She already knew that it was DJ because he was the only one that called the house phone besides Trill, and she knew they were together.

"What?" Dana yelled into the phone, ready to cuss DJ out until he asked her whether they wanted to go to the club tonight. She didn't know what to say as a cold chill came across her, thinking about how she got shot the last time she was in the club. She did want to get out of the house, and so did Tracy, so she told him they wanted to go.

"What's wrong, Dana?" Tracy asked.

"DJ just called and asked if we wanted to go to the club tonight."

"So, what's wrong? You did tell him yes, right?"

"You should already know that I did because we are tired of sitting in this damn house, but you know that I got shot the last time we went out to the club."

"Dana! Baby, them niggas are dead, and I don't think nobody else wanna take the chance of trying to kill DJ and miss again."

"I know. You're right, Tracy, but I still can't help thinking, what if somebody else does and I get hit again? I might not make it this time, Tracy. I barely made it the last time. I love DJ but don't want to die because I love him."

"So, what are you gonna do?" Tracy asked.

"Im'ma just go and try my best to stay calm and have a good time."

Damn, I hope nobody start shooting tonight! Dana said to herself.

Chapter 14
DANA

DJ and Trill arrived to pick up the women around 10 o'clock. Trill was driving while DJ was laid back in the passenger seat wearing a black hoodie shirt. It wasn't even cold enough to have the damn thing on, but he did.

Trill jumped out of the driver's seat and into the back with Tracy so Dana could drive.

Dana stepped back to admire the brand new black-on-black Cadillac Escalade with 24-inch chrome rims before jumping into the driver's seat and adjusting it because Trill had the seat laid back.

"Baby, whose truck is this?" Dana asked as she put the gear into drive, pulling off knowing she had never seen that truck before.

DJ turned and faced Dana with a serious face before replying.

"It's yours, baby. It's yours." She thought that he was joking at first, but the seriousness on his face told her otherwise. That was the only thing he said about the truck, and Dana left it at that.

"Go to the gas station down Shockoe Bottom and Broad Street!" Trill yelled from the back seat.

The Exxon gas station was the only station down Shockoe Bottom where everybody met up before or after the club. Dana wondered why they were going there.

"If you don't mind me asking, why are we going there first?" Dana asked curiously. She didn't think that DJ would answer her, but he did by telling her that they would meet up with the rest of his crew. DJ would get his Bang Squad team, and those fools live up to that name. They would bang their pistols at any and everybody, knowing that they were going made Dana feel a whole lot safer because she knew they would kill anybody trying to hurt DJ or Trill, and being that she and Tracy are their women, they would also kill for them.

"DJ got his army for us tonight, so I'm safe." Dana finished thinking to herself.

B. MILLER

DJ

DJ knew Dana would be worried about returning to the club, so he brought his whole crew with them. She knew DJ and Trill could handle their own, but it would have been hard to protect her and Tracy when it's two niggas against a whole neighborhood.

"Baby!" He called out to her. "Everything is gonna be alright," he told her, then turned the volume up on the Carter III album on the Apple Music displayed on the dashboard's computer screen. He wanted her to hear the sound system he had installed in the truck for her due to the factory sound system not being sufficient.

He had bought the truck for Dana because he turned her car into a straight-up trap car, plus he wanted his lady to ride in style.

"We shining, Baby," DJ thought to himself, then started laughing, thinking about what Smokey said in the movie *Friday*. *'It's Friday. We ain't go no job. We ain't got shit to do.'*

Everybody in the car looked at him like he was losing his mind. He just smiled back at them.

"I'm high as shit off of those Perk 10's!" DJ shouted, but nobody could hear him over the blasting music.

They pulled into the back of the gas station parking lot where the rest of the crew was waiting. Dana was ready to stop till DJ tapped her leg and motioned with his hand for her to keep going.

The crew followed suit filling in one car behind another. They pulled into the club's parking lot, not to mention the hottest club in Shockoe Bottom, *'The Canal Club.'* They looked like a freight train going down the street, having to be twelve cars deep with four people in a car.

The line to the club was wrapped around the building. Instead of waiting in line like everyone else, they walked straight to the front.

DJ and Trill walked together behind the women, which was a sight to see. They were both dressed alike in dresses that barely covered their asses. The only difference was Tracey's dress was white, and Dana's was black, matching the black jeans, hoodie shirt, and Timberland boots DJ had on.

"Damn, Dana's ass is Phat!" DJ thought to himself, looking at all of the weight she gained back from when she had gotten shot. The phat'ness sat in all of the right places.

"DJ, I got us," Trill said as they reached the front door where the bouncers stood. DJ nodded, keeping a straight face that nobody could see because he still had his head's hood pulled down low.

After Trill paid the bouncers, they waltzed inside the club without even being checked. If they had been checked, the bouncers would have found the two .40 caliber handguns DJ had under his shirt.

Soon as the doors to the club opened, the weed mixed with tobacco smell flooded their noses. To the right of them sat a bar with a food stand at the far end of it. There were a few tables in the center of the floor where a few couples sat eating and
drinking, but the real party was upstairs.

They went through a side door to the left and up a flight of stairs, with the weed smoke getting stronger with every step they took. Soon as they reached the top of the stairs, they went through another door, coming out where the party was jumping. Everybody at the two pool tables to the right stopped playing and watching the game to see who they were.

A little past the pool table sat the upstairs bar where DJ and his crew headed. The women stopped at a railing in the center of the club so you could look over and see the tables downstairs where they came into the club.

"Stay in our eyesight!" DJ told them before heading to the bar. It seemed like everybody in the club was showing them mad love. Everywhere they turned, people were trying to give them dap or stop to holla at them.

While DJ and Trill stood at the bar waiting on their drinks, they watched and laughed at their young bucks acting a fool on the dance floor.

Women were all over Trill even though he tried to play the cut. Tall as he was and sporting the bright yellow Gucci shirt he had on didn't help his cause. All he needed was for Tracy to see the flock of women surrounding him, and all hell would break loose. To make matters worse, he couldn't even hide with the bright Gucci shirt he had on with blue jeans with yellow on the pockets and custom-made Air Force One's to match his outfit. When it came to dressing, DJ and Trill were like night and day. All of DJ's clothing was name brand, but where Trill chose to wear bright colors, and DJ liked all dark colors.

After receiving their drinks, they headed to the picture booth to flick it up. Dream, Slim, and the rest of their O.C.U. Squad clique was already over there, flicking it up when they walked up. They were acting like fools throwing money around, pouring drinks down females' shirts, just straight wilding out. DJ loved to party with them because they set it off by having a good time wherever they went.

"Yo DJ!" Dream hollered. "Y'all niggas come and flick it up 'wit us. If a nigga ain't with one of our crews, they're not taking pictures tonight." Dream yelled over the music, throwing more money in the air.

DJ and Dream brought out the picture man and just as Dream said, nobody else was taking any pictures, niggas were mad but weren't stupid enough to try and start no shit. DJ's crew along with Dream's crew, niggas weren't trying to die...fo'real.

DANA

Dana took a few pictures with DJ and them but ended up finding a seat in a booth beside the picture booth to watch DJ. Every time DJ, Slimm, and Dream got together, they acted a fool. From what she had heard, they all went to school together, and even though they were from different blocks, they always kept in touch, showed each other respect, and would ride for each other if the time ever came. Whenever Dream and Slimm were around, they always brought out a part of DJ that few people could. With them, DJ was like a kid, throwing money around, straight hyped up, whereas most of the time, he was always serious except around Dana and Trill.

He noticed Dana sitting by herself, sipping her drink, and started to make his way over to her.

"What's wrong, baby?" He asked as he approached the table.

"Nothing. I'm good. Just watching y'all over there acting crazy."

"Are you sure you're good?" DJ questioned. "We can leave if you want to!"

"No, baby. We don't have to leave. I'm good fo'real. I enjoy watching all of you fools," Dana replied, then started laughing.

"Slide over then. Im'ma chill 'wit you. I'm always 'wit my niggas."

"Yeah, you got that right!" Dana thought to herself, trying not to start anything in the club.

Even though she didn't want to start anything, DJ thought the exact opposite, with his hand going up under Dana's dress. Little did he know, he was in for a big surprise. When he reached the spot where her thong should've been, he looked at her, shocked, before asking,

"Where the hell are your panties at?"

Dana smiled at him while closing her eyes as he parted her pussy lips, sliding one of his fingers into her already moist womanhood.

"Damn, that shit feels good!" She said it a little louder than she intended to. As she started to relax, DJ stopped.

"Why did you stop?" She whined, opening her eyes and witnessing the commotion on the other side of the picture booth.

Trill walked up with Tracy sliding into the booth opposite her and DJ.

"Girl, what's going on?" Dana asked Tracy, trying to whisper.

"Girrrl, Dream and them over there arguing with the West End niggas, and both sides are deep as hell with their guns out," Tracy replied, getting hyped off of all the drama she knew was ready to jump off.

"Tracy, you know that if that shit jumps off, our men will roll with O.C.U. niggas, right?"

"Shit!" Dana mumbled. Soon as she finished telling Tracy if something jumped off, their men would be involved, Vell's gung'ho ass walked up along with the rest of the Bang Squad Crew.

Still in thought, Dana watched DJ pull guns from underneath his shirt.

"No wonder he got that hot ass hoodie on. I didn't even know he was strapped," Dana whispered to Tracy.

"Dana, Tracy...y'all get down!" Yelled DJ. "Shit is ready to hop off!"

The girls got down but stayed up just enough to see what was happening with their men. Soon as DJ stood up, Dream shot one of the guys in the face. After that, the club scene turned into the Matrix.

DJ started shooting his guns into the crowd non-discriminately at anyone on the opposite side of Dream, not caring who got hit.

"That boy is crazy!" Dana yelled to Tracy as she watched Vell jump onto a table with a gun that looked like it could be a MAC 10, and knowing him, it probably was.

Trill laid low, covering DJ, shooting anyone who tried to run up on them.

"Fuck!" DJ yelled, ducking down, trying to take cover.

"Vell, go get Dream. He just got hit!" DJ hollered, letting off more shots into the crowd.

As soon as Vell jumped off the table to get Dream, Dream jumped back up, yelling.

"Y'all niggas can't kill me!" he shouted and started shooting again.

Trill grabbed Tracy and Dana to move towards the front door. DJ was walking, shooting niggas like he was invincible and couldn't get hit, and picking up other people that got shotguns along the way.

The entire shoot-out frightened Dana yet excited her at the same time. She was scared shitless, heart racing as bullets flew by, but as she watched DJ in action, taking control, it turned her on simultaneously.

Dream had one arm wrapped around Vell's neck while shooting with the other, moving through the crowd like he wasn't even hit.

DJ...Out for Blood

Trill and Tracy left the club to get the car, while Dana stayed beside DJ, afraid to leave his side. She knew that he would have given his last breath before he let anything happen to her. When they made it outside, cars were lined up waiting on them. You could still hear gunshots ringing in the distance, but it didn't matter to them. They vaulted to the cars and left.

DJ

DJ laid back in the passenger seat, thinking about how shit got so out of control. Tonight, was supposed to be his chill night, not to go out and shoot the whole damn club up. He wasn't mad with Dream, though, because he knew Dream would have held him down the same way, but he didn't want Dana in the mix because she was still trying to recover from when she got shot. Then to make matters worse, Dream got hit, and even though he looked alright, the blood soaked into his shirt said differently.

"Pull over right here!" DJ told trill, then jumped out of the truck before it came to a complete stop. Trill followed his lead, also asking,

"What's up?"

"Im'ma drive yo. Go ahead and lay back."

Dana never even opened her mouth. Trill didn't say anything. He just gave DJ an 'are you sure' look, then jumped into the SUV's passenger seat. When DJ jumped back into the truck, but on the driver's side, Dana asked him if he was alright because he never drove anywhere. DJ ignored the question, scrolling on the dashboard screen until he came to Waka Flocka.

DJ had so many thoughts going through his head that he didn't know what he wanted to do first.

Slim took Dream with him, so DJ knew that he was in good hands and should be straight, but somebody needed to take care of the war that had just started.

"Dana, slide that bag underneath your seat up here!" DJ called out as he stopped at a red light.

Trill looked over at DJ, turned the music down, and asked him,

"What's good? You got that look in your eyes, my nigga."

DJ assured him that he was alright, and once again, Trill didn't believe him. DJ made a right onto Main Street, then another right onto Eighteenth Street and park. Party goers were standing around the pizza shop on the corner of Eighteenth and Main Street, one of the many hangout spots after the clubs let out. You could tell something else was ready to jump off. It was like you could feel the violence in the air. Everybody was standing around in groups waiting for anything to spark the already hot coal.

DJ grabbed his Ruger Mini-14 Tactical Rifle from the bag Dana had just slid to him and jumped out of the truck. Niggas were playing games that he didn't have time to play while talking shit that he didn't have time to talk. His boy had just been shot, and a lot of niggas were going to DIE behind it. That's how he felt.

When everyone noticed DJ walking towards them, a few hid behind cars knowing what was ready to happen, while others tried to pull their guns out, but DJ already had his out, cocked, and ready. He opened fire on everyone, even a few people from his hood. "Any and everybody can get it!" He thought, ducking behind a car to switch up the gun clips. DJ paused for a second, looking up at the police car that just pulled up beside him.

"Shit!" he cursed, wondering how he let the police get the drop on him. "Fuck it! This cracker is gonna just have to kill me, but he better do it before I get this other clip in." DJ mumbled to himself putting another clip in his gun not caring if the pigs were right there.

BOOM! BOOM! BOOM! BOOM!

DJ jumped and tried to get out of the way, thinking the police were shooting at him until he heard someone calling out his name.

"DJ! DJ, let's go!" Vell yelled out to him.

DJ had forgotten Vell was following them when they left the club but was happy that he was. DJ put the extra clip into the Mini-14 and let off a spray of bullets while running back to the truck. Soon as DJ jumped into the SUV on the passenger side, Trill pulled off. DJ didn't even have to tell him to get in the driver's seat. Trill already knew because DJ trained him well.

"Yo, did y'all see Vell?" DJ asked, still hyped up and talking to no one in particular.

"Yeah, we saw his stupid ass!" answered Dana. "What the hell is wrong with him? He shot a cop!"

"The fucking Pig had the drop on me. Vell did what he was supposed to do!" DJ yelled, defending his lil man.

"DJ, y'all have to stop all this crazy shit before someone ends up dead or in prison for life!" Dana yelled back, with tears falling from her eyes. DJ didn't even respond to Dana's comment. He didn't feel like hearing her preach all night. All it did was go into one ear and right out the other.

"So, where are we going?" Trill asked.

"It's on y'all!" DJ answered. "Y'all wanna get something to eat?"

"NO!" Both of the women said at the same time.

"I don't want to be involved in no more shootouts tonight!" Dana said.

"Shit, neither do I!" DJ thought before saying, "fuck it, let's go home!"

It took them about ten minutes to get home which seemed quicker. Everybody was lost in their thoughts. They didn't even have the music playing anymore.

Trill and Tracy walked home. Dana went into the house to her and DJ's bedroom while DJ sat in the living room cleaning the Mini-14, looking at the news, and taking shots of Vodka.

Even though he was busy with what he was doing, his mind was on Dana. He knew that she wanted the best for him but being in the streets making money is what he loved to do. Dana acted like he wasn't in the streets before he went to prison, plus she knew what she was getting herself into before she got with DJ.

"Fuck!" DJ mumbled as he thought about Dana.

"Am I falling for her? Naw, I can't be! I mean, I do have feelings for her but not enough to change for her.

"DJ," Dana called to him as she walked into the living room, snapping him out of his thoughts. She had changed her clothes from her club dress to a red silk night shirt that stopped right above her knees.

DJ couldn't help but wonder if she had on anything under her shirt. Knowing her, she didn't, he thought. Sitting there thinking about her being nude under that nightshirt gave him an instant hard-on.

"Yeah, Baby, what's up?" he asked, turning the Tv to another new channel.

"Look, DJ! I'm not trying to tell you what or what not to do, but you know y'all as in you and Trill will have to stop all of that shoot'em up bang bang mess. I love you, DJ!" Dana walked over to him.

"And I can't help but sometimes think, what if you happen to get shot one day or even killed? That shit will crush me, your mother, and your daughter."

"Since you've been home, how much time have you spent with your daughter?" Dana asked.

She's right! DJ thought. He hadn't been spending any time with his daughter or any of his family for that matter. DJ bought her daughter anything she wanted or needed, but he knew it was more to being a father than just buying things. He was the only natural parent his daughter had besides his mother because his mother wasn't shit. She never spent time with or bought her anything, so Dana was right. He had to start thinking about more than just himself and his crew.

"Yeah, you're right!" DJ said, pulling Dana onto his lap.

"Soooo, you're not gonna try and argue with me?" Dana said, surprised.

"Naw, baby. When you're right, you're right!" answered DJ.
"There is no need for me to argue with you when I'm the one that's wrong."

"Tell me this, though?! Did you see your man in the club getting his thing off, handling two guns like a pro?" DJ asked, changing the subject.

DJ...Out for Blood

"How couldn't I see you out there acting like a damn maniac, like you were in the damn jungle somewhere."

"Dana, don't front like you don't like that crazy shit!"

"I don't like to see people get shot!" She shot back while massaging his shaft. "But I love that street part of you, the way you throw niggas around." With that said, Dana dropped down to her knees and started giving DJ some of the best head he's ever had. With his eyes rolled into the back of his head, all DJ could think was, "Yeah, I'm falling for her!"

Chapter 15
DANA

For the last few weeks, after Dana had talked to DJ about spending time with his family, he started coming into the house early to spend time with her and his daughter instead of hanging out in the streets all night. Now you all know that saying, when everything is going good, something bad is bound to happen. So, here goes the bullshit.

DJ and Dana were chillin' in the house watching TV when someone came banging at their door. They both thought that the police had finally come to get DJ, but when Dana went and looked through the peephole, she saw Tracy outside crying. When she yanked the door open, Tracy barged into the house hysterically, just straight going off. Dana guessed when DJ heard Tracy and not the cops; he came into the hallway to investigate what Tracy was hollering and yelling about.

"Tracy! Tracy!" Dana called out to her while grabbing onto both her arms, trying to get her to calm down.

"What's wrong, Tracy?" Dana asked, hugging her and starting to cry now herself, hating to see her best friend the way she was. It seemed as though when Dana let Tracy into the house, she became even more dramatic, crying, falling out on the floor, and yelling. You name it, and she was doing it.

"D...D...DJ! They shot Trill!" she blurted out in between sobs. Dana's entire body stiffened up, hearing that Trill got shot. She just knew that she couldn't have heard Tracy right. She looked over at DJ, standing in the middle of the floor. He quickly paused in front of them as if in a daze. Whatever he was feeling, he didn't show it, which scared the shit out of Dana.

"This nigga is too calm!" She thought, which should have been a good thing being that he wasn't going off.. But in actuality it wasn't for him anyway.

Dana just sat in the middle of the floor, still holding Tracy, staring up at DJ, while thinking to herself.

I've seen this nigga go off over small stuff. Look at how he acted when Dream got shot. Now his best friend, brother, son, whatever you wanna call Trill to him has been shot, and he's calm? Naw, he's not gonna fool me like that!

DJ

When DJ heard Tracy come into the house yelling, he was pretty sure the cops weren't there to lock him up but figured she had come to talk to Dana about something Trill had done. He went into the hallway to tell Tracy to shut all that damn noise up and to find out what the hell Trill had done now, but he wasn't prepared for Tracy to tell him that Trill had been shot.

Hearing those words sent cold chills through his whole body, and his mind filled up with rage once the chills left. Dana half carried, half dragged Tracy up the stairs to their guest bathroom to try and calm her down while DJ went into their bedroom to make some phone calls.

Vell was the first person he called because he had eight missed calls from him. DJ had turned off all of the ringers to the phones so that he and Dana could chill out together without any interruptions, which he felt was a bad mistake on his behalf.

Vell said they were standing in front of his house, the one that DJ gave him, grinding when a Sky Blue Cutlass pulled up and started shooting at them. They knew how the ambulance and police took their time responding to calls in the hood, so they took Trill to MCV Hospital themselves, where they were still waiting to find out if Trill was going to make it.

"Stay there!" DJ screamed. "Me and the girls are on the way! If y'all can, find out who the fuck drives that car and who shot Trill!" With that being said, DJ hung up the phone without waiting for a response.

DJ...Out for Blood

"Dana, y'all come on so we can go to the hospital!" DJ yelled, then walked out of the front door. *If they don't hurry up, Im'ma leave their asses!*

It took DJ less than five minutes to get to the hospital because he ran every red light on the way there. As soon as he walked through the front door with the women, they were greeted by no one other than Detective Anderson with a big Kool-Aid smile.

"DJ, my main man. What's shaken' Baby?" Anderson smiled, asking sarcastically.

"What the fuck's so funny?" DJ asked back, ready to beat the silly grin off of the detective's face.

"Boy, you better watch who the fuck you are talking to like that before you end up like your boy in there!" Anderson replied through clenched teeth, real low so that DJ would be the only one to hear him.

DJ was tired of letting Detective Anderson get away with stuff, tired of his mouth and letting their beef slide because killing a cop is a DEATH SENTENCE if you got caught, but now he figured it was time for him to think about killing Anderson.

He knew that if he was going to kill Anderson, he had to be smart about it and catch him where he thinks he's safe...his house! To find out where the Detective lived, he needed Jessie. He could find out where anybody lived, and as soon as DJ left the hospital, he would pay Jessie a visit.

"Baby," Dana called out, "come on. This is not the time

nor the place, plus he's a pig." Dana rubbed DJ's arm while pulling him towards Vell and the rest of their crew.

"Shit, the crew!" DJ thought. Vell had everybody there. DJ couldn't see how he hadn't noticed them when he first walked into the hospital. It had to be at least twenty-five of them there. He was glad that the dumb-ass detective didn't try anything stupid because he and the whole crew would have been in jail. Vell would have followed his lead, and the crew would have followed Vell.

"Yeah, shit would have gotten hectic in here!" DJ mumbled.

"Vell, what's good my nigga? Have y'all heard anything from the doctors yet?" DJ asked, giving him some dap along 'wit the rest of their crew.

"Yeah, the doctor said he's gonna survive," said Vell. "He got hit once in the right shoulder and once in the right side. He's still in surgery right now, but he should be out soon," Vell said, telling DJ everything the doctor had told him.

"Dana, you and Tracy stay here so when Trill comes out of surgery, someone will be there with him and call me as soon as he comes out!" DJ kissed Dana on the head and walked off without waiting for a response. Dana just watched him walk off, knowing that there wasn't anything that she could say or do to stop him from leaving.

DJ...Out for Blood

Chapter 16
DJ

DJ drove to the hood to pick up one of his guns and some perks he had stashed at Vell's house, then to the store to get a bottle of juice to wash the pills down. He needed to clear his head because he was in a bad mood, and destruction was on his mind, so he drove around the city for a few hours. Dana had sent a text message that Trill was in stable condition and out of surgery because DJ didn't answer the phone when she called his phone. He didn't feel like talking to anybody, especially Dana being that all he could think about was that his lil nigga could have died today while he was in the house laid up boo-loving with her.

DJ rode around with the music off, talking to himself as if someone else was in the SUV with him.

"Bitch ass niggas know what it is 'wit me! They know that they just started a war fo'real now!" DJ yelled like a madman while hitting the steering wheel.

"Trill is my right-hand man, so niggas know I'm gonna retaliate. I have to be smart about this because Detective Anderson will come after me before anybody else. Especially since he already has it out for me," DJ said in a low, calm voice.

"Naw fuck that!" He growled out, hitting the steering wheel again. "I'm going after him first. Kill or be killed bitch! You should've killed me, Anderson!" DJ yelled out as if Detective Anderson could hear him.

He pulled out his cell phone, called Old Head Jessie, and told him to open his front door because he was about to pull up out front.

"A yo! Get me Anderson's address!" DJ said soon as he walked through the front door.

"Anderson!" Jessie replied. "I know you are not talking about Detective Anderson, are you?" Jessie asked, surprised, knowing that's who DJ was talking about but still not believing he was hearing him right.

"You know that I'm talking about Detective Anderson!" DJ snapped. "Why are you acting all surprised and shit?" DJ asked looking at Jessie suspiciously.

"It's just that I've been telling you that you needed to get rid of that asshole, but you always refuse to listen, always saying that same thing every time," Jess answered over his shoulder while walking into a back room.

"Yeah, yeah, yeah. I know…DEATH PENALTY! And I still feel the same way too!" DJ replied.

That is why nobody knows I'm gonna do this, DJ said to himself. One thing Jessie always reminded him from his early teachings was never to let your right hand know what your left hand was doing. That's why DJ never told anybody what he was ready to do.

"Here it is," Jessie said, walking back into the living room.

"When do you plan on doing it?" Jessie asked.

"Why? What does it matter to you?" DJ asked, ignoring Jessie's question and asking one of his own.

DJ never let Jessie know that he knew that he and Detective Anderson were the ones who set him up to go to prison. He played everything cool so Jessie could help him get back on his feet, and now that he was doing well for himself, he could have his revenge. "Payback is a bitch!"

Jessie was excellent at what he did, teaching DJ well, but he had no loyalty to anyone but himself, which is why he will not lose his life.

"It doesn't matter. I was just asking, that's all." Jessie answered not starting to get scared.

"Naw, you weren't just asking! You were asking so that you could warn Anderson when I was coming." DJ pulled out his gun and pulled the hammer back on it.

"Yeah, I thought we were better than this too, but you? You, Jessie, broke our fucking bond!" Yelled DJ. "I looked up to you, and you crossed me! Naw, this can't be forgotten or forgiven." With that said, DJ quickly shot Jessie twice in the chest and once in the head before he decided against it and let Jessie live. Jessie was dead before he hit the floor. Those RIP bullets coughed out of DJ's gun sending him immediately to R.I.P. DJ rushed out of the house just in case somebody heard the shots and called the police. He drove for a few blocks before pulling over and parking so that he could grieve a little over the loss of Jessie. Even though he didn't show any emotions to Jessie, it hurt him deep down to kill him. The man was like a father to him.

When DJ's birth father died, Jessie stepped up to fill the void, teaching DJ how to make money and survive in the streets, but he also taught him that when a person broke the codes of the streets, it was a MUST that they are dealt with accordingly. Jessie broke one of the codes by snitching, so DJ dealt with him. Jessie was now just part of collateral damage. Now DJ has to deal with Detective Anderson.

Chapter 17
DJ

Detective Anderson lives on the outskirts of Richmond, about forty-five miles out West Broad Street, in a small town called Centerville.

The entire town was mostly made up of farms and corn fields, which was suitable for DJ because it made it easier for him. The Detective's house sat off the main street down a dirt road with a cornfield to the left and woods surrounding the rest of the house.

DJ pulled right up in front of the door to see if anyone answered it. He already had his mind set on killing whoever opened the door and anybody else inside the house. When he didn't get an answer, he pulled his truck around the back of the house, parking as close as he could near the woods. Everything was pitch black back there, so nobody could see the truck unless they pulled their car around the back of the house and the car headlights happened to catch it. To ensure he had the drop on anybody parked in front or back of the house, DJ laid down in the grass on the side of the house.

DJ knew that he was taking a BIG chance being there because he wasn't even sure if Detective Anderson was coming home tonight. Would somebody be with him if he did, or what time would he even get there? And if he did come home, it was a chance DJ was willing to take and patiently wait out. With a wicked grin, DJ cocked his gun. *I have to stay on point and do this right. No gun, no witness, no case.* He said over and over and over, knowing that one slip would cost him his life.

DANA

Dana left Tracy at the hospital to be with Trill after he came out of surgery so that she could go home and get some rest. She had to take a taxi because DJ had taken the truck, leaving her without a way to get home. She tried to call him a few times but figured that the phone was powered off because it kept going straight to voicemail.

On the ride home, she kept hoping she would catch DJ there and confirm that he wasn't, which she already knew. Soon as she walked into the house, Dana went straight to the bathroom to take a hot bath to try to relax and ease the migraine she had from worrying about DJ. She didn't know what to do or to think about Trill getting shot. Dana knew that DJ wasn't in the right frame of mind, not thinking straight, and was liable to do anything at any given time to anybody that he might figure had something to do with the shooting.

Dana loved DJ to death but hated that he wouldn't let her inside his head and be there for him. She had been in love with him since she was a teenager, and now that she finally had him, she was not ready to lose him.

She lay in the tub crying, needing someone to talk to. The only person she could talk to is her best friend, Tracy, but she was still upset about Trill getting shot, leaving Dana alone with her thoughts.

For the first time in her life, Dana felt isolated. Even with her parents being dead, she always had Tracy by her side and now that Tracy had her priorities to deal with, Dana had nobody else but DJ to rely on, who she couldn't find.

Tears began falling down Dana's face causing her to say a silent prayer to God, asking Him to keep DJ safe and to bring him home to her. Before dozing off to sleep in the tub, Dana mumbled, "Baby, please come back home to me!"

DJ

It was after two o'clock in the morning when DJ arrived home. He walked into the house and straight to the kitchen to make a strong shot of gin. DJ needed to relax and get his thoughts together. DJ felt terrible about killing Jessie even though he had broken the code of the streets. But he still has to worry about Detective Anderson.

He had waited hours for the detective to come home, and Anderson had three other officers with him when he did. DJ had to use his willpower not to try to take all four of them out. His blood boiled inside of his body as he clutched his gun. He was already taking a BIG risk by being there and it would have been an even more significant risk trying to take on all four of the cops.

DJ thought about trying to take Anderson out when he ran into his house alone, but after a few minutes, he decided against it. He knew the other cops would come running once they heard the gunshots, so he just watched and waited until they left before driving himself home. DJ knew he would pay Detective Anderson another visit sooner than later.

DJ gulped down his drink and then poured himself another one. Hearing a noise coming from upstairs for a second time, he pulled out his gun and took it off safety while easing towards the stairs.

The first time he had heard the noise, he just brushed it off, figuring his mind was playing tricks on him. But the second one was loud and clear, sounding like something fell and thumped on the floor.

He first checked the guest bed and bathrooms before walking into his room. As he entered the room, he noticed a light glowing from underneath the bathroom door. He stooped down as low as he could get as he eased open the door to the pitch-black room.

He took a deep breath before going into the bathroom gun first. He stood up, relieved when he saw Dana in the bathtub asleep. The glowing light was from a candle that she had burning sitting on the sink. The candle was new, so DJ could tell that she had been in the tub for a while, being that it was almost melted away.

He grabbed Dana's towel from the towel rack on the back of the bathroom door and then let the water out of the tub before picking her up into his arms and getting himself wet in the process. She jumped a little when he first touched her wet skin but quickly relaxed once she noticed it was DJ.

DJ sat down on the toilet seat with Dana still snugged inside his arms, then wrapped her in the towel. Her body was cold and wrinkled from being in the water for so long.

"Hey, baby!" Dana whispered into DJ's ear while wrapping her arms around his neck.

DJ didn't respond. He just looked down at her, trying to figure out how he fell so deeply in love with this woman.

He looked over at his gun that sat down on the sink's granite countertop, then back at Dana. One part of him felt it was her fault that Trill got shot. If he hadn't been in the house hugged up with her, he would have been out there with Trill, but deep down in his heart, he knew that wasn't true.

"Baby, what's wrong?" Dana asked, wanting to know why DJ

stared at her so hard.

She sat up, putting one leg on each side of him. Once again, DJ didn't respond. Instead, he bent down and started kissing her. He worked his way to the nape of her neck, taking in the sweet aroma of french vanilla coming from her body, and then to her beast, sucking on the one at a time. Dana released a soft moan as DJ gently bit down on her nipples.

"Damn baby, I love you!" Dana whispered into DJ's ear before sucking on it. DJ slid his pants down, using one of his legs to get them off while massaging one of her breasts and sucking on the other.

She pulled DJ's already hard dick out of his boxer shorts and straddled him. She was a lil tight at first, so DJ didn't go all the way in, but the more she rose and went back down, the deeper he went and the wetter she got.

He picked Dana up, carried her over to the sink countertop, put one of her legs over his shoulder, and started taking long strokes. He would pull almost all the way out and then ram himself back into her.

"Whose pussy is this?" DJ asked each time he rammed himself inside of her.

"Huh? Who's it!?"

"It's yours, baby!" Dana screamed back. "She's always been yours!"

"DJ, right there, baby! Stay right there! Owww, this shit feels good! Fuck me, DJ! Fuck me harder!" Dana yelled out in pleasure.

"D…DJ…I'm cum…cumming, baby! Please cum with me!" she

cried out in between breaths.

DJ didn't respond. He pumped harder and faster until they released themselves—her on him and him inside of her.

He just stood there for a moment before putting her leg down and then grabbing a washcloth so he could wipe both of them off. When he finished, he picked Dana up, taking her over to their bed, where she fell asleep in his arms.

Chapter 18
DJ

"Dana! Dana. Wake up!" DJ said, shaking her.

"What's wrong DJ?" Dana asked, wiping her eyes and then looking over at the clock, noticing that it wasn't even eight o'clock in the morning yet.

"Get up so we can go check on Trill," he answered, then walked out of the room.

"Shit!" Dana mumble. She didn't feel like getting up this early in the morning. She wanted to lay and relax, plus her body was still sore from the sex DJ had put on her.

DJ went downstairs to fix Dana some breakfast. He knew that if he didn't, it would be at least another hour before they left the house.

Twenty minutes later, Dana emerged from upstairs, down into the kitchen where DJ is making her plate of food.

"You're not gonna eat, baby?" Dana asked when DJ put both of the bacon, egg, and cheese sandwiches he made onto her plate.

"Naw, I'm good. Im'ma get something later," he replied before telling her to bring her food and then walking out the front door.

"What's good, my nigga?" DJ asked soon as he walked through Trill's room door at the hospital.

"What's up bra?" Trill grumbled back.

"Tracy, Dana is outside in the front waiting on you. She's gonna take you home to change clothes and to get some food."

"A'ight!" Tracy replied. She kissed Trill before walking out of the room, telling Trill she would see him later.

"So, how're you feeling, Dawg?" DJ asked, getting serious now that Tracy was gone.

"I'm good Dawg! Sore as hell, but I'm good." Trill answered trying to sit up some.

"Did you find out who shot me?"

"Naw, Dawg. The squad is on it, though, and as soon as we find out...were' going to war!"

"Dawg, I thought I was gonna die when that bullet hit me. That shit burned like hell. It felt like my insides were on fire."

"I'm sorry Dawg," DJ said, holding back the tears in his eyes.

"Sorry? Sorry for what?" Trill asked, trying to figure out what DJ was talking about.

"I should've been there with you, Dawg. If I hadn't been in the house hugged 'wit Dana, I would have been out there 'wit you." DJ answered, wiping his eyes.

"DJ, you can't blame yourself for what happened. One, I'm a grown-ass man, and you can't be with me at all times, and two, you're not bulletproof. Think about it, Dawg! You might have been killed if you had been out there. I'm good, my nigga. Believe that!"

"My nigga, you're right, but I still can't help feeling like I should've been with you. I even thought about smoking Dana last night. To be real, I almost did because if it wasn't for her, I would have been out there with you."

"Dawg, you're trippin' fo'real! You know that Dana loves you, and

I know that you damn sure love her, so stop blaming her and yourself for what happened to me. There isn't shit that you could've done, DJ, so get that crazy shit out of your head!"

"Yeah, you're right, Dawg. I might not have been able to stop niggas from shooting you, but I'll tell you this…they will regret it."

Deep down inside, DJ knew what Trill said was right, and he also knew that if he had killed Dana, he might never have come out of his depressive mood.

"I know they will DJ. I know they will!" Trill replied.

DJ...Out for Blood

DANA

"Girl, you know whoever shot Trill 'don started some shit!" Dana said, taking a sip of her orange juice.

When Tracy and Dana left the hospital, Dana took Tracy to McDonald's to get some breakfast and to give the boys some time to talk.

"Yeah, I know, and that's what scares me. You know that DJ will go overboard because it was Trill who got shot."

Dana slumped down in the chair she was sitting in and stared out the window, thinking about what Tracy had just said.

"Dana, what's wrong?" Tracy asked, noticing the change in Dana's mood.

"I think that DJ blames me for him not being out there 'wit Trill."

"Hell, naw Dana! Why would you even think that?" Tracy asked, shocked.

"Dana, DJ might be a crazy, cold-hearted bastard, but when it comes to you…there is no doubt in my mind that he loves you and would never blame you for anything like that," Tracy replied in DJ's defense, not believing the words that just came out of Dana's mouth.

"And that's the problem right there!" Dana exclaimed, trying not to cry.

"Hold on for a second. You've lost me, sis. I'm really not following you right now."

"Listen, Tracy. I know that DJ loves you, and that love is what had him in the house with me when Trill got shot instead of out there with him." Dana expressed, taking another sip of her juice.

"Ok. I understand that, but I can't understand why he would blame you?" Tracy stated.

"Because I'm the one who told him he needed to start spending more time at home."

Dana went on to tell Tracy how DJ found her asleep in the bathtub the night before, picked her up out of it into his arms, and sat down on the toilet seat while still holding her in his arms.

"Awwww, that's so sweet!" Tracy said, putting both of her hands over her heart.

"Sweet! Tracy, I thought that fool was going to kill me!"

"Kill you? Yeah right! I can just picture DJ killing *you* 'wit your legs in the air. Let me find out you're paranoid!" Tracy began laughing, just knowing Dana had to be joking.

"Tracy, if you could've seen how he was looking at me, you would've felt the same way."

"So, what happened after he looked at you funny?" Tracy questioned.

"He made love to me," Dana shot back, half telling the truth.

"He made love to you?!" Tracy said a little louder than she intended making a few of the customers stare at them.

"Can you just be a little bit louder?" Dana asked, trying to be sarcastic.

"Dana, I'm sorry, but listen to how you sound!"

"I know, I know. It sounds crazy. You just had to be there to see how DJ looked at me and that damn gun."

"Excuse me, ladies." Two men tried interrupting them.

"We're already taken," Tracy retorted, dismissing the two men who had just walked up on them, thinking that the men were trying to get their holla on.

"Listen BITCH! Don't nobody want y'all hoes? We have a message for your men."

Hearing the mention of their 'men,' Dana and Tracy both looked up and directly into the face of the notorious Fat Daddy. They both immediately recognize him as one of the West End boys that Dream got into with at the club.

Dana reached into her purse sitting on her lap and wrapped her fingers around the .40 caliber pistol that DJ had left sitting on the bathroom sink the night before.

"And the message is??" Tracy asked, rolling her eyes.

"Tell that nigga Trill that he lucked up and lived this time, but the next time, he won't be so lucky and tell DJ He's next!"

"Nigga, you got the game fucked up if you think Im'ma let you threaten my man!" Dana said, speaking up for the first time, pulling the gun out, cocking it, and putting it between Fat Daddy's legs.

"Bitch! You're not crazy enough to shoot me with all of these witnesses!"

"Now, see…that's where you're wrong at. Before I let you hurt DJ, I will kill you right here, right now." Dana teased with the gun locked on his manhood as she got up from her seat. Tracy didn't know what had come over her. She just knew that she meant every word she said from the look in her eyes. Slowly, Fat Daddy backed up, still running his mouth, trying to be tough. But deep down inside, he felt that Dana would shoot him if he stayed. Once Fat daddy and his boy just stood there saying nothing, Dana put the gun back inside her pocketbook and sat back down.

Tracy was in disbelief at what had just happened.

"Girl, what in the hell is wrong with you?" Tracy asked, still shocked that dana pulled out a gun on Fat Daddy.

"Tracy, nobody is going to be threatening my man! And I mean NOBODY!"

"Yeah, y'all are made for each other because both of you are nut cases! *Nobody is going to be threatening my man, and I mean nobody,*" Tracy said, mimicking Dana

"You just sat here talking about you thought that DJ was gonna kill you last night, but now you are pulling guns out like you're Queen Latifah in *Set It Off.* Then you talking about ain't nobody gonna be threatening your man. Where in the hell did you even get a gun? I know DJ didn't give it to you."

"So, how did you get it?"

"Well, after we got into the bed, I played like I was exhausted and fell asleep, then once he fell asleep, I slipped out of bed, got the gun, put it in my purse, and got back into bed like I never got out of it."

"Girl, your ass is crazy fo-real! Come on, and let's get out of here in case somebody calls the police." Tracy said, noticing people watching them, mumbling amongst themselves.

DJ

DJ sat outside the hospital inside the truck, listening to all the details of what transpired at McDonald's. Dana told him everything from her taking his gun to her pulling it out on Fat Daddy, only leaving out the part about when and why she took his gun.

DJ didn't know what to say or do, so he just sat quietly, listening, biting down on the inside of his jaw. Part of him was mad that Dana took his gun, but the other part was happy that she did and glad to know that if it ever came down to it, she would put in that work to protect him.

He knew exactly who Fat Daddy was and planned on dealing with him soon. He wasn't mad that Fat Daddy threatened him, but he violated when he shot Trill and stepped to Dana, talking mad shit.

DJ couldn't figure out why Fat Daddy came at him and Trill first, not Dream. He knew that Dream was still laying low until his gunshot wound healed, but his boys were still out there.

"Dana, pull off," DJ barked out, turning to look out of the rear window cocking his gun that he took back from her.

"Where are we going?" she asked pulling off as instructed.

"Just ride around for a few!" he replied, turning back in his seat, now looking out of his window into the side view mirror.

"What's going on, DJ?" Dana asked, looking back and forth from him to the road.

"I'm trying to make sure this nigga ain't following us!"

"Why do you think that?"

"If he knows that you're my woman, he knows that you will run straight to me and tell me what happened and lead him straight to me or our house."

"Make a left right here, then pull over to the left," DJ told Dana as he rolled down the window.

Dana decided to keep quiet; generally, she'd be shooting out question after question. But she chose to remain silent and follow directions. She knew it wasn't the right time to tell DJ to calm down. A few seconds later, they watched as a sky-blue Cutlass bent the corner and sped right past them. Dana let out a breath she didn't realize she was holding as she waited for the gunshots to go off.

"Pull off," DJ said calmly as he watched Fat Daddy cruise down the street, trying to find out where he went.

"Don't lose him, Dana!" DJ said, looking around to ensure there weren't any police.

"Pull up right beside him. I wanna catch his bitch ass off guard," DJ said while grabbing the door handle and clutching the gun in his other hand.

Dana whipped the SUV around fat Daddy's car so he would be on DJ's side. Before she made a complete stop, DJ jumped out of the vehicle with his gun aimed directly at Fat Daddy.

"Bitch, I heard that you were looking for me!"

"Nigga, fuck you!" Fat Daddy yelled back, not caring that DJ had a gun pointing at him. All he knew was that DJ had better kill him, or he would kill DJ the first chance he got.

DJ replied by letting off two shots, hitting Fat Daddy in the chest.

"Arguhhh! Shit!" Fat Daddy hollered, losing all of his toughness he had at first and now gone.

"Come on, DJ man. Don't kill me!" he begged as blood began spilling from his upper torso.

"Naw nigga. Fuck me remember!" DJ yelled back, hitting him two more times in the chest. "Now it's fuck you!"

"DJ! Come on!" Dana shouted out, scared that somebody had seen him.

DJ jumped back into the truck, laid back in his seat, and closed his eyes as his new partner in crime drove away from the crime scene with Fat Daddy's voice playing over and over in her head of him begging for his life.

Chapter 19
DANA

~KNOCK! KNOCK! KNOCK! KNOCK!

~BANG! BANG! BANG! BANG!

"Who the hell is it!?" Dana yelled, running to see who was banging at the front door.

~BANG, BANG, BANG, BANG!

Dana yanked open the front door without looking through the peephole to see who was banging at the door. Now standing in front of her was no other than Detective Anderson. His fist almost hit Dana in the face, not realizing that she had opened the door while he was still banging on it.

"What!?" Dana shouted, not bothering to hide her attitude toward his presence.

"Where is DJ!?" His anger was overly present.

"Why?" Dana fired back.

"Ms. Davis, I don't have time for this shit! Now where the hell is he?" Detective Anderson yelled.

"Look, Dee-tec-tive," sarcastically, Dana began. "If you don't have a warrant, I suggest you get the hell off my property!" Dana spat out as she tried to close the door, but Detective Anderson placed his foot between the bottom of the door to prevent Dana from closing it.

"Oh fuck, Nah!" Anderson screamed out before he tried to barge his way into the house. Dana stood her ground by putting her foot behind the bottom part of the door to keep it from opening up.

"Listen bitch! I know that DJ shot Fat Daddy and you were there with him, so you can either tell me where DJ is at, or both of you are going down for attempted murder!"

Dana thought her heart skipped a few beats when she heard Anderson say attempt murder. Fat Daddy isn't 'dead?' she thought to herself. But how? She watched DJ kill him, so he had to be dead.

Detective Anderson noticed her facial expression change and realized that she and DJ didn't know that Fat Daddy was still alive. Upon seeing this, Detective Anderson used this newly found information to teach her.

"Oh, what? You all thought he was dead?" Anderson asked with a smirk, now covering his face.

"Tell DJ to call me, or I'm gonna make sure both of y'all are locked away in a dark hold for the next twenty years." Detective Anderson turned around and left, knowing DJ would pay him to stay out of jail. He just knew that he now had DJ right where he wanted him, and with that being said, he already played right into his hands.

Nobody ever knew that Detective Anderson and Fat Daddy were best friends. They had grown up together out in Henrico County. When DJ jumped into the beef between Fat Daddy and Dream, and Anderson heard about it from his best friend, he saw an opportunity to get DJ.

Detective Anderson had set the entire thing up by first getting Trill shot and then having Fat Daddy step to Dana, knowing that DJ would go after him when he found out.

DJ...Out for Blood

Anderson and Fat Daddy knew they were playing a dangerous game going at DJ, hoping that he wouldn't take any headshots because if he had, Fat Daddy would have been dead, and the bulletproof vest wouldn't have kept him alive.

Dana watched as the detective strolled to his car, not believing anything he just said or not wanting to believe none of it for that matter. Her head felt like it was doing black flips and would burst open at any moment. It had been a week since DJ shot Fat Daddy, and they both thought he was dead. Shit, it took her the whole week to get the memory of him begging for his life out of her mind, and he wasn't even dead.

Dana knew that shit was ready to get out of control, and she was smack dead in the middle of the drama. After learning this information, she knew she had to quickly go back to the bedroom to wake up DJ and tell him what the detective had said. No sooner than she closed the front door, DJ stepped from behind it with his gun out, causing her to jump back until she noticed it was him.

DJ

"I was just coming to wake you up!" goes Dana. "How long have you been standing there?"

"Long enough," answered DJ.

"So, did you hear everything Anderson just said?"

"Yeah, almost everything," he said, tucking the gun into his waistband.

"So, what are we gonna do, DJ? I'm not trying to go to jail. I can't do it!" Dana yelled out, frantic.

"We? We are not going to do anything. I will handle it," DJ answered, walking into the living room. He needed a drink and fast to ease the pending migraine he was feeling.

DJ knew that he had messed up big time, so he didn't even check the news to ensure Fat Daddy was dead.

"Damn!" he mumbled, sitting down on the couch, picking up the bottle of gin he had sitting on the table, and taking a long swig of it straight from the bottle.

Dana followed behind him, sitting down next to him on the couch. She wanted to know what he was gonna do about Anderson and Fat daddy. She needed him to ease her mind because she was so nervous about going to prison for accessory to murder that she couldn't keep her hands from shaking.

"Here, drink some of this alcohol. It'll calm you down some!" DJ said, handing Dana the bottle of Seagram's 102-proof gin.

"Tomorrow, I'm sending you, Trill, and Tracy to the Bahamas.

DJ...Out for Blood

All of y'all need a break, especially Trill since he just got out of the hospital yesterday."

"DJ, you know we are not gonna leave you here by yourself!" Dana whined, trying not to let the tears fall from her eyes.

DJ pulled her into a tight embrace and whispered into her ear that everything was gonna be alright.

"How do you know, DJ? What makes you so sure?" dana asked, with her head resting on his shoulder, still clutching the bottle of gen in her hand.

"Listen, baby. I can't tell you what I'm going to do. That's not something that you need to know. If the police ever question you, you can answer them truthfully about not knowing anything. I messed up by having you out there when I shot Fat daddy, and I knew I shouldn't have had you there. So, please, baby, just relax and let me handle this."

He never did answer dana's questions. The truth was that he really couldn't answer them, not truthfully anyway. He had never lied to Dana before, so he avoided the questions as best he could.

Chapter 20
DANA

"It's so beautiful out here!" Tracy blurted out, staring at the clear blue water. Tracy, Dana, and Trill arrived in Nassau, the Bahamas, around 2 p.m. They headed straight for the beach because they didn't bring any luggage. When they packed, they brought only one book bag each to not cast any suspicion if they were to have been traveling with nothing. Trill has his own money to pay for his and Tracy's way, while DJ still paid for everything for everybody.

Dana nor Trill responded to Tracy's comment. They were both lost in their thoughts. They just laid back on the oversized beach towels they had brought on their way to the beach.

Dana dug her manicured toes into the silky sand as she wondered if DJ was ok or not. She knew that he could handle himself, but with her and Trill not being there with him, there wasn't anybody there to make him think rationally, meaning that he was liable to do anything at any given time.

She looked over at her best friend, looking out at the ocean, excited to be in the Bahamas, which Dana wished she had been before, but neither one of them had ever been outside of Richmond before, but without DJ being there, she couldn't enjoy herself.

"Are you alright, Trill?" Dana asked, looking toward him. Trill had wanted to stay in Richmond with DJ, but he was still in bad shape from getting shot. He had to move in slow motion so the staples in his stomach wouldn't burst open. She knew he was still mad from the argument he and DJ had before boarding the plane.

"Yeah, I'm good," Trill answered in a groggy voice, apparently from the pain medications he had been prescribed after being shot in the stomach.

"Trill, you know you couldn't have stayed, not in your condition."

"Yeah, I know, but he still could've waited."

"Trill, it cou—"

"Look, I know y'all are not going to mope around here all day!" Tracy butted in, cutting Dana off in mid-sentence.

"Both of you know that DJ can handle himself, plus he got those damn young fools from around Ladies Mile Road along with Dream and his crew behind him.

Both Trill and Dana turned and looked at Tracy. She couldn't understand how they felt because she didn't have the same kind of relationship with DJ that they did. Then if you let her tell it, couldn't nobody go up against DJ and win? Not even an army.

"What? Why are y'all looking at me like that?" Tracy asked, wishing she would have never even opened her mouth. She knew they would twist her words and take them as something she didn't mean.

"How long are we supposed to be down here?" Trill asked.

"Until DJ sends word that everything is safe," replied Dana.

"Until he sends word? What the hell is that supposed to mean? What about a phone call or something!" Trill became agitated.

"To be honest, Trill, we might as well get comfortable and try to enjoy ourselves like Tracy said because we might be here for a while."

"Well, in that case, y'all can go ahead. Im'ma just lay back right here and try to clear my mind. I can't get into the water anyway."

"Baby, are you sure? I don't wanna leave you here alone," Tracy said, getting up off her towel.

"Yeah, I'm sure. Just don't be all day!"

"We won't brotha! We're just gonna get in the water for a while, and then we can go shopping later," Dana replied.

DJ...Out for Blood

DJ

"Big bro, gimme the word, and I'll dead them both for you!" Vell slurred.

"Naw, lil homie. We have to play this one smart. We can get the gas chamber for killing Detective Anderson even though he's a dirty cop," DJ responded after taking down one of the shots of liquor he had sitting in front of him.

After sending Dana, Trill, and Tracy to the Bahamas, DJ set up a meeting with Dream and his crew. To ensure his family was safe, he sent his mother and daughter to Disney World for two weeks, then went to pick up Vell.

It hurt him to send Trill away at this time, but he couldn't protect himself and Trill when the bullets started flying. Fat Daddy not only had a strong crew behind him, but he had the police behind him as well.

While Vell and him sat at Apple Bee's waiting on Dream, they sat at the bar taking shots of Vodka while discussing what needed to be done with the detective.

"DJ, you already know I'm 'wit you all the way. It doesn't matter what we have to do or who we have to go up against."

DJ knew that Vell meant every word that he spoke. He had already proved his loyalty on different occasions more than once.

"Yeah, I know, my nigga. That's why you're here 'wit me."

Dream walked into the restaurant with at least twenty other guys surrounding him like they owned the place. His crew was falling out of the group two at a time, sitting at tables throughout the restaurant to have all angles covered so they could see who entered the place. One would've thought that the President of the United States stepped in how they walked in.

"DJ, Vell, what's good?" Dream said as he turned to the bartender to order himself a drink. After the bartender handed Dream a bottle of Grey Goose, he turned his attention back to DJ.

"So, what's the problem?" Dream asked.

"Fat Daddy!"

"Fat Daddy?" Dreamed questioned, "I thought you smoked that fool!" he whispered.

"Well, I didn't. The nigga had on a bulletproof vest."

"Damn, DJ. I'm surprised you didn't shoot him in the head." Dream was shocked, being that headshots were DJ's specialties.

"So, what's the problem? Just go find that nigga and hit his ass again." Dreamed spoke as a matter of fact.

"That nigga has Detective Anderson working 'wit him. I need to go at both of them at the same time. I can't take the chance of letting one of them get away."

"I'm going after Anderson! I got something special planned for him. I need your squad to kidnap Fat Daddy, and we can go at his crew. Every time one of them shows their face, I want it blown the fuck off. It's a must that all of you keep Fat Daddy alive.

"Say no more, my nigga. It's done! When do you wanna hit them?" Dream asked, taking a sip of the drink he'd been nursing.

"Friday night! I wanna start knocking them niggas off.

You know they're gonna be on the club scene like every other week."

"Then Friday it is!" Dream stated, looking over at Vell with a mischievous smile. Dream just smiled back, knowing that when DJ let Vell loose, it was going to be a blood bath in the streets.

Friday night, Club 321 was jammed packed. It seemed as though the whole city had come out to party. Dream planned to throw the party at the club to ensure Fat Daddy and his crew came out.

DJ, along 'wit Vell, sat parked across the street from the club, watching everyone that went and waiting for them to show their faces.

"How do we supposed to get these into the club?" Vell asked, pointing at the .357 and army knife sitting in his lap.

"The bouncers work for Dream. He's not gonna search us. Just follow my lead," DJ responded, pulling off the Black-n-Mild cigar he was smoking.

"Oh shit! That's detective Anderson right there!" Vell yelled, pointing at the detective walking across the street to the club.

"Yeah, I see him, and that's Fat Daddy's crew walking behind him, but I don't see Fat Daddy anywhere in sight."

DJ waited a few minutes before entering the club behind Anderson and Fat Daddy's crew. He hadn't expected to see the detective at the club, so he had to be extra careful. Vell followed DJ, watching everybody that came their way. He had his hand tightly gripping the army knife as they walked through the smoke-
filled room to a booth.

It was hard for them to tell who was who because the club was jam-packed with dim lights. DJ planned on using the dim lights and smoke to his advantage to move around the club without being seen.

"DJ, you can't afford to be seen, so Im'ma go roam around and take a visual inventory to see where everybody's at. You chill till I get back."

DJ looked at Vell, contemplating what he had just said before nodding his head in approval. He watched Vell as he walked through the crowd with his fitted baseball cap that matched his own pulled down as far as it would go on his head and disappeared in the smoke.

DJ...Out for Blood

DANA

"Come on, brotha! Have a little fun!" Dana said excitedly to Trill. They were now out shopping for clothes and other necessary accessories that they needed for their getaway time on the Caribbean Island. Trill dragged behind the women, still pissed off that he couldn't have stayed with DJ.

Trill knew he should have been trying to make the best of their situation, but he just couldn't get in the mood.

"I am having fun!" Trill blandly replied, but the women knew otherwise.

"Liar! Come on now Big Brother. How do we suppose to enjoy ourselves with you moping around here?"

"Look, once we get back to the rooms, y'all can leave me there and go about y'all's business."

"Come on, Trill. Don't act like that!"

"Dana, let his silly ass stay in the room alone if he wants to!" Tracy butted in.

"Tracy, this ain't the time," Trill replied, giving her a stern look.

"Y'all, please don't start. I'm trying to enjoy myself. Trill, you know just as well as I do that DJ can handle himself. Don't get me wrong, I'm still worried about him because I know that anything can happen, and he's not bulletproof, but I'm pretty sure he is alright with Vell holding him down."

Trill contemplated over what Dana was saying for a few seconds before responding.

"Yeah, I guess you're right lil sis."

"Nigga, you know I'm right! Before Vell lets something happen to either of them, he will try to kill everybody around them."

Trill smiled for the first time since DJ told him he was sending them out of town. He knew that if DJ was safe 'wit anybody besides himself, it was Vell, plus he trained Vell just as DJ had trained him…maybe better.

DJ...Out for Blood

DJ

"This is from DJ, pussy!" Vell whispered into Anderson's ear.

Detective Anderson stood frozen as he felt Vell's hot breath on his earlobe before plunging the army knife into his chest. Anderson tried to grab the knife, but Vell quickly twisted it counterclockwise, rendering the detective hopeless. Vell then yanked the knife out of his chest, causing Detective Anderson to bleed out immediately. He then did two quick and fast jabs in the throat. Vell backed up as blood began squirting out of the wound, sending Anderson to the floor, grabbing his neck and flopping around like a fish. Calmy, Vell turned around and walked away in search of DJ.

"I got him, Bra!" Vell yelled to DJ as he approached the table he left DJ sitting at.

"What?" DJ asked, not hearing what Vell said over the loud music.

"I said I got him! Anderson is a done deal!"

"That easy?" DJ was shocked at how fast and efficiently Vell got Anderson.

"The nigga was slipping Bra. He must have thought his ass couldn't be touched, and that's where he fucked up."

DJ knew that if Vell said he got him, he got him. It just surprised him how easy it was. He looked around and noticed the commotion coming from the back of the club.

"That must be where Vell left Anderson at." DJ thought to himself.

Club goers started leaving the scene once they noticed the body flopping around on the floor, and it sure as hell wasn't someone trying to break dance. A sudden panic spread throughout the club, and everybody started rushing for the door simultaneously, with screams echoing in the background.

DJ and Vell sat at their table watching everything unfold, not wanting to leave before the paramedics pronounced Anderson dead.

"Chill right here for a second," DJ said, getting up and walking off.

Vell sat back and watched as DJ maneuvered his way through the crowd to where Anderson lay wiggling on the floor.

DJ looked down at Anderson and smiled before pulling out his gun and shooting Anderson in the head. Calmly, he turned around, heading back towards Vell.

"Now he's dead! Let's roll!"

Vell shook his head and laughed as he followed DJ out of the club. *Pow! Pow! Pow! Pow!*

"DJ, get down!" Vell yelled, spinning around with his gun out, trying to find where the shots came from. The shots stopped just as fast as they started within a split second.

"DJ! DJ! Come on. Get up Bra! DJ, get up!" Vell gave DJ the once-over look and noticed the blood soaking through the back of his shirt.

"Naw Bra! Not you. Come on, DJ! You can't die on me!"

When Vell heard the police sirens approaching them, he started searching DJ, taking the gun off him that he shot Anderson with.

DJ...Out for Blood

"I swear, Im'ma avenge you Bra!" Vell whispered into DJ's ear before running off, disappearing into the night, praying that his big homie didn't die.

TO BE CONTINUED...

Made in the USA
Middletown, DE
21 July 2024

57496626R00092